Moltenrose

Two Stories and Two Poems
from the *Pale Zenith* Universe

Wendy Rathbone

In a post-holocaust world, a young woman and her robot partner leave their nomadic gang to take a long trek on foot to the city of Moltenrose to seek their fortune. **Green Forever** is a coming of age novella about love, death and making your own luck.

In the story **Moltenrose**, a deformed man whose nickname is 'Ugly' lives in the shadowed ruins of the barely-alive city and works in a sideshow at the tourist-trap carnival at the edge of town. His story involves several 'firsts' including a lesson about beauty.

For Della

who came back from the dead

Moltenrose

Contents

Green Forever

I. The Edge

On the morning of Green Forever, the spring equinox, Sarine left her sisters, her five-year-old son, all her friends of the Wolf-Spiders, and headed on foot for civilization. Sterling went with her. He trudged in the wake of her dust, faultlessly loyal, found companion who never aged, though rust now and then had to be scraped from his heart.

It had been hard leaving. Tyranny, her son, had cried and cried, and Sarine had had to push him away, rough, because she felt that would be easier on him in the long-run. Though she'd resigned herself to be alone, to start a new life far away, she had been broken by the final good-bye.

Sterling was silent as Sarine pushed to the hills, through sand like broken glass, across crumbled foundations of the houses destroyed in the Seven-Day War. A century had come and gone since that devastation, and still the air smelled acrid, and the sky seemed to reflect it with an ever-present yellow haze.

Her water bottle sloshed against her back as she walked. Kicked sand glinted, settled in minute waves behind her. Sterling's metal feet crunched ash with mineral.

We walk on bones, she thought as they passed the bent and blackened handlebars of an old tricycle.

Green Forever's breeze journeyed cool. Sarine's long, albino-white hair played at curls against her pack. She liked the feel of it down and tangled, and when it got too matted and fused, Sterling would trim and comb it to submission.

At dusk they stopped and Sarine erected their bubble—a stolen piece of technology not unlike Sterling—her bounty from one of hundreds of raids on other gangs, on country towns, on trans-hop lines. The auburn bubble sprouted from a single coin-sized disk. Inside, already assembled, was an attached air-mattress. The bubble was not only warm, but bullet and flame proof. She and Sterling would sleep secure.

Under the evening stars, like broken glass on tar, Sarine sparred with Sterling, keeping in practice. The job she hoped for, security in the city of Moltenrose required a fighter. Her desert-fighting techniques had to be perfect.

The rolling hills to the south sent oceanic shadows toward them. In the distance, ruins served as pretend sentinels. The crescent moon rose late, a ladle of silver dipping into the night.

Sarine absorbed it all into her mental conditioning, her physical reflexes, and became wolf, spider, lizard, crow, defeating Sterling through surprise and technique more than strength.

Later, Sarine slept, dreaming of Tyranny. Sterling slept, dreaming of nothing.

*

On the second day of Green Forever, Sarine saw a flash of white light on the horizon. A trans-hop with its caterpillar-like formation traveled to the southeast. She headed in that direction, hoping to follow its tracks. One of its stops had to be Moltenrose. Though the city was mostly a ghost-town, one end of it had gone over to tourism. But she was headed for the other end: a zone of ruins that lapped the skin of a silver tower stretching, rocket-shaped, into the sky. It was that tower that called her. Though she'd not be living in it, the special inhabitants needed protection. The job-opening specified a guardian-angel position. It paid well, and she'd have the run of the streets.

An hour later, Sterling found the single, shining trans-hop rail they wanted to follow. His red eyes seemed to glow brighter as he said, "Here, Sarine. Here."

"Good," she replied, smiling up at his metal face.

His lips were the softest part of him—except for his genitals—and they quirked in a return grimace, his version of grinning. He lived to please her. It gave him a reason to exist as all sentient creatures, especially 'created' ones, needed.

Sarine's own reasons for living were human enough, but unsatisfying. She was brought up on deterministic views—*we were meant to take this, steal that, fight her, love him, or we wouldn't be here, capable, with all this dangling in our faces*—but that kind of thinking gave her no pleasure. At least Sterling appeared to take pleasure from his reasons, which included acts as small as her smile. Could it be that easy?

The sand turned browner as they walked, and foliage started cropping up: stick weeds like skeletons, thorn patches the color of blood, tiny-furred cactus that looked alive.

"We are coming out of the Edge of the World," Sterling said.

"Yes. But we should still look sharp for gangs."

"Always."

An attack could come from any angle at any time. With her learned gang-sense, Sarine could predict their strategies, smell them from miles off. So far, nothing moved in their direction but the fading afternoon light bouncing rainbows off the trans-hop track. Off Sterling. Off the metal bio-pacer Sarine wore on her wrist to keep psychotronic forces aimed randomly at her country nullified. The price of war was that small bracelet. She'd had it since she was born, and a spare taken off a dead Comet-grazer—rival gang to the Wolf-Spiders—rode under the water bottles in her pack. At any time, she knew, her bracelet might be stolen in an attack, or broken in an accident. The spare was necessary.

Sarine shuddered, lengthened her stride.

"I'm glad it's Green Forever now," Sterling commented, his shadow thrown long on the sand, as human as hers in shape, in gait. "My favorite time."

"Why do you think that's so?" Sarine asked. She'd still never managed to uncover where he'd come from. He'd either been erased, or truly forgotten. He didn't even know how old he was. She had trouble thinking of him as a machine. He was so soft-spoken, so kind. It complemented her roughness. Statements of emotion were common from him.

"New life," he replied, after a moment's hesitation. "That is beauty defined. And truth." He seemed to sigh, a breath holding a small, metallic wheeze. "I don't know why I say these things."

Sarine laughed. "I don't know either."

"But they please you?"

She touched his arm. So cold, as all of him was. She'd touched him everywhere, when she first found him, to be sure, and he hadn't minded. In fact, he had imprinted on her ever since. "You please me," and she tightened her grip wondering if he noticed, though he insisted he did 'feel'.

Just before sunset, Sterling's keen eyesight noticed motion from a mile away.

"Animal?" Sarine asked.

"Human."

"What else do you see?"

Sterling scanned, red eyes deepening to almost-black. She could hear things going on in his head, sounds that reminded her of a bird's warble, or a delicate, flowing stream.

"Male," he finally answered. "Armed."

"Keep an eye on him. We're taking a detour."

The ground was still flat, the foliage thin, so there was little cover to be found. But Sarine and Sterling headed away from the trans-hop rail, hoping he would pass by without seeing them. It was getting dark, and Sarine needed to set up the bubble soon. She did not want strangers anywhere near her campsite.

"Too late," Sterling said. "He's seen us. He's coming our way."

"Not a smart one. He doesn't even know what we are."

"Perhaps a desperate man, then." Sterling's voice held a note of anxiety.

Sarine swung her pack off and fished for her scorebeam. A dark tube with a handle, it held pulses of fire that could scorch or, on the highest setting, kill. "Take this." He handed it to Sterling. Then she checked her knife, sheathed and fastened to her thigh within easy reach.

When the stranger was about a hundred feet away, he called out. "Hello."

Sarine had already known as much as Sterling could tell her with his eyes. That he was armed—Sterling's vision detected a scorebeam in a deep, jacket pocket—and that he was tired-looking, weary, dressed in torn vinyl and moth-eaten fur. "What do you want? You should know better than to approach strangers out here near the Edge."

"Kill me, then," he said noncommittally. He had long, black hair, shaved on the sides as was the fashion, though the sides had partially grown back, fuzzy and curly. The rest was braided and hung over his left, synthi-fur-vested shoulder. His skin was brown, like her own eyes, and he was tall.

"If I don't, a gang surely will," Sarine said.

The man took a step forward, shrugging. "I'm lonely. Death is crowded. I'll go willingly."

Immediately, Sarine scanned his arm for a bio-pacer. His behavior reminded her too much of psycho-madness. The war, fought psionically by psychics, affected all whose minds were not protected. She saw the strip of metal on his wrist and frowned. Not madness. Then what?

"You wish to die?" Sterling called out, startling Sarine with the boldness of his words.

"No such thing as wishes," came the answer, the man still ambling forward. Seventy-five feet now, the sand hollowing under his boots. The sky narrowed from blue to pink. A sudden scent of jasmine, alien, unseen, gathered about them on the breeze. "Ah, smell that?" he cried. "Where is that coming from? I'd love to see that plant!"

Sarine felt the scent enter her and open her up. Something, a memory, tried to get free. When Tyranny had been born, she's smelled jasmine. When her best friend, Marri, had been stabbed through the throat by a Comet-grazer, she'd smelled jasmine again. Jasmine meant only those two things to her.

"Stop," she called. "Stop right there."

He hesitated, took another step forward. He had to be only sixty feet off now.

"You're armed. I'll shoot."

"Me?" He frowned, dark eyebrows like painted lines edging toward each other above the bridge of his nose. "Oh, yeah. My scorebeam. Never use the thing except to cook with."

Fifty feet.

"Take it out slowly and throw it on the ground."

"Whatever." He sounded bored. A tactic Sarine knew better than to believe. But he obeyed, kicking the tube to the side, not even looking back at it. "Well," he said, at twenty feet, scowling at Sterling. "I thought you looked different from a distance. Are you really a toy-droid?"

Sterling moved the scorebeam an inch higher. "I'm not familiar with your term."

"Pardon me. It's slang, of course. I meant no offense. You're much more than a machine. Toy-droid is therefore derogatory."

"What do you want?" Sarine demanded.

The man shrugged. Fifteen feet. "Nothing but maybe a shared cook fire? I'm heading for my brother's out in Lonetown. It's a long walk. I had no money for a trans-hop."

He made her nervous. Strangers with no fear out on the Edge or beyond could mean nothing good. Yet he was no longer armed.

"Aren't you afraid we'll kill you?"

Ten feet. "Then kill me. You can have everything I own. It doesn't matter to me."

He was crazy, but his eyes were calm. At fifteen feet, he'd stopped. She could see his teeth were white and strong. He'd been someone worth something once to be able to afford dentistry. Her own teeth were straight, but had never been so white.

"You're suicidal then," she observed.

He bowed his head. His breath sounded strong behind the breeze, resigned. "Just tired of being afraid all the time."

"Being afraid and being stupid are different," she pointed out.

"If you'd been more than two people alone, I would not have approached."

She squinted in disapproval. "Keep the gun on him," she said to Sterling.

"Sure."

She approached, hand out. "Give me your pack. Let's see what you have."

Without preamble, he handed it over. It was loose-woven blue plastic, new-looking. The contents included water, mini-meals that expanded when exposed to the air, a solar battery-powered library no bigger than her hand, a solar blanket. Her own supplies of nuts, dried beef, and some dehydrated fruits and vegetables seemed rustic in comparison. Her only technological convenience was the bubble...and, of course, Sterling. In the bottom of the pack she saw he had a bubble, too. The gold coin nestled in the plastic seams.

She looked up. "Is that mini-food good?"

"Try some," he offered. There were at least fifty small packets.

She was tempted. With Sterling to keep an eye on him—and herself an adept fighter—it seemed safe. "I'll try one. But if it's poison, Sterling here will kill you."

"It's not poison," he said, a string of fur flapping out from his arm like a flag. "Try the library, too. It's great."

"I don't read."

"Oh." He said no more, but sat as Sarine placed his pack on the ground and went to sit closer to her own.

Over dinner, he said his name was Grath and he'd come from Caritte, one of the largest cities on the Peri ocean. He was as soft-spoken as Sterling, almost too calm, and talked about schools and studying all subjects, and books, books, books. "I got tried," he said. "Years of reading made me restless. Instead of just reading about other people having adventures, I decided to take off to meet my own destiny."

"You said you were headed for Lonetown. Is that your destiny?" Sterling asked.

"Maybe. I don't know."

"You were like Sarine was before she left her family on the Edge," Sterling said. "Believing your destiny comes to you. But now you seek it."

"Exactly," Grath said. "You understand this?"

"Like you, I'm self-programming. Only I am aware of it."

Grath blinked, confused, dark eyes shimmering in starlight whites and campfire golds. Then his eyebrows rose. He smiled. "Hey, that's pretty good."

Sterling shrugged. "It's my truth."

Sarine nodded once, licking her teeth. "He knows a lot. Maybe as much as your library there, but in different ways."

"I have no memories of books," Sterling admitted.

"Everything is a book if you look at it long enough," Grath said. "You don't need them, perhaps, for your journey. Me, I can't imagine life without them." His teeth touched his lower lip, pinching it into his mouth.

Sarine had little to say, but her feelings were crowded and strong. He intrigued her, this craziness of his startling but new. She'd set out for something new, a job, another life, but strangers were going to be the hardest new thing to accept.

14

She saw enemies everywhere. Gang paranoia. Having Sterling along alleviated the condition somewhat, but the need to survive was so strong she felt compelled to strike before struck. Even after sharing food, after seeing that Grath's scorebeam was retrieved and hidden by Sterling, her mind produced scenario after scenario involving Grath's death at her hand. She was strong enough to strangle him in his sleep. Or cave in his chest with a kick. Or burn off his head with her own scorebeam. But none of the images called for completion.

His burnished skin gleamed. She liked that about him, the warm coloring. It reminded her of beautiful Marri whose skin had been almost as dark. Who had died at fifteen with a knife in the throat.

Sarine had become used to death after twenty-one years gang-bred and raised, but not the acrid taste it brought to her mouth. The taste of pain. The taste of metal and blood. The thought brought back Grath's words when she'd threatened him on approach: "Then kill me. It doesn't matter."

"Did the books make you unafraid of death?" she asked.

His face, open and alive, their small fire throwing auburn shadows upon it, widened in a smile. "I said I was tired of being afraid. It doesn't do you a bit of good if fear keeps you from experience."

"Did you learn that from books?"

His smile did not falter. "A little."

Sterling said, "I would think fear would keep a person from making a deadly mistake."

"Or it could kill them," Grath replied. "Common sense keeps people alive. Fear keeps people ignorant. *That* I learned from people."

"Hmm." Sterling placed a piece of scrap wood on the fire, tinder that exploded in deep orange flecked with green. The smoke smelled faintly of creosote.

Sarine stared at the flames, remembering Marri's eyes, wild and all-whites as they fluttered and she fell, her lips forming the word "No" as she drowned in her own blood.

"I'm afraid of death," Sarine said. *And insanity from this war fought with mind-altering transmissions that come on invisible winds.* She fingered her bio-pacer bracelet.

"It's in us all. Like another realm." Grath scratched his right ear. "You can deny it or not. It doesn't change."

"I don't believe that." Sarine glanced at Sterling who stared at nothing but flames with red-light eyes that danced hot. "There has to be a way around. I'll find it."

"What if the only way is through?"

Sarine didn't answer, her muscles tense. She was beginning to hate this conversation.

"There is so much more than what we see," Grath stated after a moment.

Sarine thought he might have made a good priest. Some gangs revered priests. Some killed them. She'd heard of priests who had seen beyond, who climbed in and out of this world as though walking through doors of an elaborate structure. She'd never met one. "Like what?" she asked.

"Other dimensions. Other worlds. The technology that fights this war we're in comes from everywhere, not just what we see."

"I don't believe it."

"You've never heard of the machines that can leap time?"

"I have," Sterling said quickly. "It's true. The spychiatrists."

Sarine gulped hard, feeling her muscles ache. She liked what she could touch, could hit, could crush. "How do they do that?" Then, before she got an answer, "Why?"

"I don't know how. But why they do it, well, it isn't enough for some people to just accept what they see. It isn't enough for me." Grath stared upward as the moon came up, a thicker ladle tonight, and gorging on stars.

16

*

Sarine lay against Sterling, her vinyl shirt packed between them like a pillow so her own warm body wouldn't absorb his cold. He was still as stone, breathing in soft, constant hisses, existing in a mechanized physicality, but real, very much alive.

They'd left Grath stargazing by the fire. Sarine hoped he'd be gone when they woke. She didn't want the complication of him right now. She only wanted to go to Moltenrose and try out for the job. Start over before she lost her youth. Twenty-one wasn't old, but it was too old for the kid-gang she'd belonged to.

Why should age matter? She wondered. But she hadn't thought of that when her other, older friends had left the Wolf-Spiders. Only now that she'd left did she wonder if the count really made a difference at all.

Sterling, separate from life, non-human but functioning as human, didn't age. The rules for him were shadowy, unlined. He was just as good a friend as Marri had been, and responded to her like energetic Tan, father of Tyranny and long gone from the Wolf-Spiders before Tyranny had been born.

When Sarine finally slept, the moon was high. She dreamed she walked lost in another world, her bio-pace missing.

*

Sterling always woke when she did, as if sensing her inner rhythms with his own machine tides. He smiled at her with his soft, silver lips, touched cold fingers to her white hair.

She saw a shadow move outside. Grath had not left, and she emerged from her bubble with her scorebeam drawn.

He pretended not to notice, kicking at cold ash from their campfire with the toe of his boot.

"What is it you want?" she asked, Sterling coming out to stand by her side.

"Well, I thought I'd ask to come along with you for awhile. If you don't mind," he said, still kicking at the gray wood.

"But we aren't headed in the same direction."

"Lonetown'll still be there…later. I have no firm plans." He glanced to the side, briefly meeting her eyes with a clear, rested gaze.

"What is it you want?" she asked again, teeth gritted.

He frowned, shook back his long, black braid. "Nothing, really."

"Everyone wants something."

Sterling made a sidestep to her right, reflecting dusk sand and blue sky and buttery sun.

Sarine lowered her scorebeam. "Even he," he said, nodding in Sterling's direction as the android collapsed their bubble into its easy-to-carry coin size, "wants something in the end."

Sterling looked up, the coin glittering gold in his silver palm. "To belong. To please," he said calmly.

"That's probably the truest and best of human desires," Grath said.

"And you claim to have none?" Sterling asked before Sarine could speak again.

"At the moment." Grath shrugged, fingered the straps of his pack which was already shouldered, vinyl incasing fur.

How long had he been ready to go? Sarine wondered. She felt afraid, and yet Grath projected a strangely likeable mood. Again she was reminded of Marri. They had run well together, partners in raids, partners in games. But Sarine didn't need another Marri. She had Sterling now.

The Green Forever wind blew, and that distinct jasmine scent came again, furrowing on the air, into her nostrils and

18

lungs. Life. Death. Both awaited her, like it or not. Existence. She hadn't joined the Touchstones or any of the other adult gangs for the simple reason that she'd wanted to find her own way for a change, and not maneuver to someone else's destiny, someone else's story. If Grath came, would her story become his, then, and not her own?

"I'll share my food and my library," Grath said, standing against pale, morning sky, a figure strange, dark, yet complacent.

She took a deep breath, still faintly jasmine scented but cool, clean. She felt rested. Uncharacteristically generous. For now. "All right."

On the journey, it was hard to shut him up; he was so full of his library and his education. Sterling absorbed quietly, unperturbed. Sarine pretended indifference, but in truth, Grath fascinated and confused her. She didn't want to feel either reaction. As they walked, she kept thinking of the other worlds, the other dimensions, as Grath called them, and machines called spychiatrists that could go there. How could she not be curious?

Her desert fighting skills also taught some mediation, a seeking into inner worlds: the selves that incorporated mind, body, spirit; the *places* in the mind where you went to dream, where you stored energy, where you met yourself and learned to 'be'. She knew the stars were other suns like her own, perhaps with worlds, perhaps with people living, fighting, loving on them. But traveling time into alternate dimensions placed a new perspective before her. Everything looked smaller. Yet limitless.

For a long time, as Grath talked of more subjects than she could count, she watched Sterling, his shadow human, yet his silver body a form altogether colder. He was solid as bone, compassionate as a child. Strong. Loyal. But alien. Yet even he feared death the same as she. In that, they were united. The same.

Breaking into the conversation, she said suddenly, "Just being tired can't be your only reason for not fearing death."

Grath paused in mid-step, touched his pack-strap. "Hmm?"

"You have either very strong beliefs," she concluded, "or some kind of knowledge that makes you so...so peaceful?" She ended with a question because she wasn't sure the last word defined what she meant. Marri had been that way in life, peaceful, yet when death touched her she'd lost her peace, gone reluctantly. She had not finished living yet. "Have you finished living?"

They'd come to an incline. Boulders dotted the land, some ten stories high, and they followed a path through them to meet, hopefully, the trans-hop line on the other side of the hill. The short-cut would save them another day's hike.

Shadows rested on their shoulders, cooling them. A lizard skittered straight up the side of one rock. Sterling's body darkened as the light slipped away.

"This looks like a good place to stop and rest," Grath suggested. "Let's have some water and I'll try to explain my views on death."

Lukewarm wetness swallowed, throat still dry, Sarine leaned against the chill of ancient earth-bone. That was what rocks were to her, the broken bones of a world. "Well?" she prompted, when Grath stayed silent too long.

"Death. What do I know about it," Grath stated, eyes closed.

"What *do* you know about it?" Sterling asked, not drinking. He never drank, or ate.

"I'm not indifferent, don't get me wrong. And I am afraid. Of pain. Of suffering. Of others suffering. But a teacher told me something once I'll never forget."

"What?" Sarine's impatience coiled in her chest.

Sterling's chest was silent. He didn't ask, but his red eyes on Grath were rapt.

"First, Death is always there, whether you see him or not. If we don't see him, should we be less afraid? If we do see him, should we be more afraid? You don't look at him because you're afraid. You know you'll be looking at him when you finally do die. You'll know, then, that he's there for you, it's final, it's over. And then, nothing else will matter in your future. It'll be all over. Your life."

"Death is a person?" Sarine asked softly.

"For this story. So he's there, he's looking at you, and what do you have to say for yourself? That you spent your life running? That you were afraid to do anything since he'd be lurking around every corner?"

"I would say to him," Sarine answered, "that I'm proud to have avoided him this long. My caution kept me from meeting him sooner."

"All right, then, but now you meet him. Everything else is finished. Where do you suppose you go with him?"

She shrugged. This scared her. She'd been knocked unconscious once in a fight, her fighting skills young and unperfected. When she woke, she remembered nothing of the fight, in fact, nothing of existence during or after the fight until she came to. This propensity toward non-existence fed her fear. Though she was an adept at fighting now, fear fueled her energy, and she too often lashed out uncontrolled, wild, unthinking. "No place," she finally answered.

"Then, how do you explain certain scientific discoveries of places we thought never to exist before, but do?"

"You mean dimensions, those machines..."

"That, and what my teacher further explained to me on a day I was rather depressed. I'd failed a psychology exam and wanted to do nothing but stare at a gray sky." He grinned, petting his pack which lay between his spread legs. The boulders kept the wind off them, made an area cool but not cold, and dim as emerging twilight.

"What?" Sterling said, startling Sarine. "Depression. Is that melancholy? I think I understand, but I don't..."

"Have you experienced regret, lack of control, loneliness, helplessness?"

"I have."

Sarine was always amazed when Sterling, a machine, could speak of such things as if honestly, delicately making claim to a life he could truly only think to have, wish for, imagine… Could a machine imagine? She believed Sterling could.

"Good," Grath said to Sterling, as though Sterling's answer was expected. "Then you know how I was then, my mood, my need. My teacher, who is now dead—an accident, a fall from a high ledge—explained to me about how the brain, or mind, if you prefer, works like a hologram. Do you know what a hologram is?" Now he looked at Sarine.

"I'm not uncivilized," she returned. Captured rainbow images on jewelry fascinated children. And communication brought a person to you for conversation, even though you couldn't touch them. She's seen holograms enough. "I have used a telecommunicator before." Though she didn't add, for no other reason than random fun. She knew no one who actually *had* a communicator, so if she used one, public or stolen before it could be shut off, anyone she might call would be a stranger for a prank.

"All right. Well, our brains use a holographic kind of code, like the telecommunicator. That's how we record data."

"I see holographically," Sterling put in. "And remember what I see in that way. So I am like you?"

"It would seem," Grath answered.

"What's this got to do with death?" Sarine asked.

"In the holographic code, any portion of the picture of the person can present the whole image. A fragment will suffice. This is how our mind works. It exists in no one place, but everywhere, all at once. Fragments contain the 'all' just as the larger sections contain the 'all'. We have machinery inside us that recreates images we perceive as existing outside us. Now the images are inside us, too. Everything connects. Our

22

code, the code that makes us work, like the hologram's code, enfolds everything all at once, everywhere. There are no boundaries. There is no space, no time, no matter, no mind. There is no linear reality. No cause and effect. Out of that comes the theory my teacher taught me on that day when I felt less than nothing. That there is, beyond time and space, dimensions where perhaps a universal intelligence—us, anything, everything—travels through all barriers, a free-floating consciousness, a collective mind, a cosmic soul. Some people think the universe itself is a giant hologram. You can't get lost, no matter how small you are, no matter if you are dead or alive."

"And these machines that travel, these machines used in the war, are they universal intelligence?" Sarine asked.

"I don't know. I would think yes, if everything is. Everything means anything; Sterling, this rock we're leaning against, a cloud in the sky, a sand flea. You."

She wanted to believe. Wished for it. Her heart pumping too fast, her fingers against her palms slick with sweat. If so, then Marri wasn't lost. No one was. And Sterling self-programmed beyond mechanical function. She wished she could have an awareness of it all, to see, to know for sure.

"You can determine your own reality," Grath concluded. "We decide where we go, what we do, what we see. There are no barriers. Not even death. So why be afraid?"

"All I know is here, now, us. I know hunger, pain. My goal is to avoid it."

"By choice," Grath said. "Intelligence, not fear, makes you seek to avoid suffering."

"I think I understand," Sterling quipped, his soft lips grimacing a smile. His metal fingers drew ridges in the sand at his thigh.

"I don't. Comparing a hologram to death just doesn't compare."

"I'm not comparing it to death," Grath said, "but to existence itself in any form."

Sarine got up, her muscles protesting, and shouldered her pack. "Let's just get going." If they were part of a vast, intellectual hologram, it didn't change anything.

Grath stretched his arms over his head as he stood, then bent to retrieve his pack, fur dangling. "It's getting hotter every day."

"Green Forever," Sterling said softly.

No barriers, no death, no mind. *But we feel,* Sarine thought. *We can't always control. If we determine reality, then what about those born into it? I didn't choose this. Marri didn't want to die like she did, a knife plunged into the delicate flesh of her neck.* Someone else had made that happen. Someone who took her control away.

*

Five days into the journey, Sarine still kept herself mentally distant from Grath, though Sterling got along with him well enough. She had to admit Grath was interesting, however, and her wariness had turned to shyness. 'Interesting' was not an area in which she believed she could compete. Only when she sparred with Sterling did she feel touched by something other than reality. A grace filled her then, a soft web of completion when she danced the way of the wolf or the crow.

"Fear doesn't make you move that way," Grath observed one night.

"No," she replied, spinning under starlight and a near half moon. The sky didn't arc true black, but poured a dark, pure blue over them that had the essence of a depthless wave. The horizon dipped where a distant valley and Moltenrose converged. One more day's walk and she'd know if what she wanted could be hers.

Sterling's limbs impacted with hard muscle, sinewy deflections. She moved and reacted and defended in ways that left no bruising, even from hard metal, ways that nurtured within her an energy that was all air and light and memory and knowledge. Sometimes, sparring, she had visions. She told no one of them.

Tonight she saw herself, wild white hair and eyes darker than burnt-out crystal, staring out a high window taller than she and wide as four times her arms outspread. The world sprawled a toy kingdom at her feet, people tiny as ants moving along streets, between buildings, some flashing bright as steel in the sun. She tasted, briefly, sugar; smelled sage. Something touched her back, gentle, caressing…cold.

"Sarine?" Sterling's voice, hand in the center of her back.

She blinked, turned to meet his red gaze, and saw behind him Grath's bubble and shadow within. When had he left for bed?

"Are you going to stay up all night?" Sterling asked.

She shook her head. He touched her hair, fingers tangling. "Needs a trim," he murmured.

She smiled. "All right."

In their own bubble, the faint blue night hazy through the tough, unbreakable plastic, Sterling's fingers worked through tangles. They pressed waves, trimmed ends, and split mats with the sharp edges of his fingers, retractable like cats' claws. He snipped. She breathed. There was the sharp musk of her own odor, and Sterling's cleaner, oilier smell pulsing as fresh air exchanged with old through the bubble walls. She sat on the air mattress, the surface a texture slightly more porous than that of the walls. Sterling knelt behind her, his weight perfectly balanced, the bed holding them sturdy as if it were earth itself. Her vinyls were piled on the floor, haphazard, dusty. She wore only ripped cotton shorts, a bracelet on her ankle made of braided ribbons, her bio-pacer. Her hair felt like silk wind against her neck and back.

"There," Sterling said, stiff fingers of both hands tracing her scalp from widow's peak to nape, cutters retracted. She shivered, but not from cold.

"There," he said again and, "Hey."

Cutting her hair always aroused him. His playful 'hey' was his machine way of saying, *I need; do you want?*

She turned, watching for the spark she sometimes saw behind the light that was the red of his 'eyes', his vision. The light came from indentations made to resemble eyes, the clear-glass-like curve a fake surface, all retina, no whites. Whoever sculpted him truly wanted him to look like a man. He had a modest nose, silvery hard with indentations for nostrils but no holes. His mouth was framed by generous lips, soft-textured like real skin, but silver, as if he applied generous amounts of lipstick on them when no one looked. He had a tongue, too, for talking, a voice box for a throat. The tongue was soft, but dry. He wore no clothes, ever, but had shoulder pieces like metal jewelry that fit like armor. There were two parts to the shoulder ornament that screwed down tight. Now, as she watched him, he took them off.

Underneath, the metal shone polished and pure, almost too bright to look at, clean as water. He rippled, blazing even in the dim bubble-light. The chest had sculpted musculature, and two tiny, bright nipples.

At his waist, more armor. The armor cupped him, crotch to carved navel, and unscrewed also to come away in two pieces. He had buttocks, smooth, cold satin, a mystery opening between them like a human anus. And in front, soft as his lips, less bright than the rest of him, a burnished penis of some rubbery texture neither hot nor cold and perfect for sex. He could have been some buffed angel escaped from a distant museum. Or, as Grath had implied, an exotic toy. But a toy doesn't ask for pleasure...

If he had escaped a place or person, Sarine was glad he had his freedom. Glad she had found him.

He was erect, and he touched her left breast with the barest of pressure from his cool fingers. A tingle squirmed through her body as he bent with pursed lips to take her

26

nipple between them and tease it with his tongue. Dry pleasure there, and then a damp kindling between her legs.

He knew how his coldness could startle her, and was careful to stroke her most sensitive areas with only his mouth, or his genitals.

She'd gotten used to his cold lines, the hard planes and edges like winter caught within frozen skin. Her body enfolded it so he had a warm flesh container for awhile, a human casing, a malleable guise.

When he breathed out, into her mouth, his breath smelled of iron and salt. Ear pressed to flawless curve of breastbone, slippery with her sweat—like fucking melted ice—she heard soft whirrings, a hum, a purr. He spoke her name, first in whispers; he always started slow. Then he built up to crying out, "Sarine!" like the loneliest of animal keening.

He seemed to orgasm, but nothing came out of him. Not like human males, with pale fluid that left stains, evidence of desire.

But she did for sure, shuddering hard this time, and he groaned along with her so that in the rush she held a sobbing machine, a trapped dream, an absent soul.

Afterwards, she leaned over him where he lay on his back. His red-light eyes gazed up as if unseeing. "Do you really feel it? The love, I mean. The rush?"

"Yes," he replied, lips in a satisfied grimace.

"What's it like? Tell me. Describe it."

Without hesitation, he said, "Like the first day of Green Forever, every time." He inhaled deep and as he let the breath go, she smelled faint rain.

Eyes warm, blurring, she said, "Yes. That's right."

*

II. The City of Moltenrose

The desert landscape receded to dry farmland, all of it abandoned, and Sarine, Sterling and Grath passed boarded up homesteads, ravines awash with hundred-year old automobile skeletons—twisted metal so caked with rust the original shapes could not be determined—an old road intersecting the trans-hop line. The pocked street crumbled to a darker gravel line that marked its once busy passage. The scent of tar-dust cloyed the air.

In fog-shrouded distance, the shape of the city of Moltenrose resembled a hunched, pregnant unicorn. The horn was the tower, silver-gray in the overcast light. The tail end housed the carnivals that drew tourists, peddlers, gamblers. In between, the body of the unicorn looked hard-edged, burned, broken. Gray and black weathering striped what they could see of collapsed buildings and complexes. It did not look alive. Pervading rain made the city little more than a mirage as they walked the crushed highway. *If I look away*, Sarine thought, *will it disappear?* Grath, with his hologram babble, would have said it always existed, and always will. Moltenrose was there because it had been made to be there by all kinds of people, and though it was technically a dead city, it still held life, and secreted away in its unicorn horn the valuable ones, the psi-gifted soldiers who fought and played the game of psychic battle against their enemy, the Walled City.

Sarine touched her bio-pacer, felt its warm current tickle her fingertips, and stared at the tower. *Are we your prisoners, or are you ours?* she silently asked its unseen inhabitants.

A wind picked up, offering a ubiquitous answer as it seemed to call over the desolate land "youuu" and "weee."

At the outskirts of Moltenrose, near the only trans-hop station, rain started to sparkle the pewter sky, the mutilated superstructures, the sooty streets. For awhile, the city looked spattered with diamonds, rich beyond dream, a captured

28

galaxy of stars providing the framework for roads and verandas and castles and fortresses.

If I see it, can I make it real? Sarine thought. But abruptly the rain stopped, leaving the city in unaltered ruin. Sarine felt damp and chilled; Sterling's carapaces were water-spotted.

"How can the universe be one giant hologram and not seem balanced?" Sarine asked aloud. This city had had more than its fair share of avarice and death.

Grath, walking further ahead, seemed not to hear.

Sterling turned red eyes on her.

She did not repeat herself, and shoved forward. Signs directed them to the carnivals, the tourist traps, the "Greatest Show on Earth." "Win Money!" "Prizes, Prizes, Prizes!" "World's Smallest Dog." Sterling quietly read them to her.

Sarine smelled burnt sweets cooking beneath the stronger smells of ash and rain. They went in the opposite direction, into the abandoned shadows that offered nothing but stepping stones toward the tower that glistened now, as the sun was starting to come out, scaly and iridescent and silver-green. It overlooked city limits, far-off valleys, green swells of hills. They could see the hills up the narrowed streets that climbed some dozen blocks.

"It's smaller than I thought," Sarine commented. "We could've come upon the tower from the hills."

Flanking her, Grath turned to respond, but before he could a voice unseen called, "You're not going to the tower."

They stopped. In the middle of the street they were too vulnerable, but Sarine had felt less safe walking by the broken windows and sagging doors of the ruins.

"Turn around. You tourists aren't welcome here!" It was the same voice but it had moved in the brief pause. First it seemed to come from behind. Now it spoke ahead and to the left where a narrow alley between cracked walls snaked into dimness. Old storefronts, windows broken out to look like huge, fanged mouths, guarded either side of the street.

"We're not tourists," Sarine called out. "I'm here to apply for the guard job. These are my…" She hesitated, glanced from Sterling to Grath, then concluded. "…my assistants."

For a moment, the wind, the air, the very essence of the ruined city itself seemed to freeze. An unnatural quiet rested over them. Sterling turned, an abrupt jerk, to his right, and the motion, a sound of metal softly scraping, echoed off the dead buildings. Grath's quick intake of breath made a hiss. And then the shadows between and within the broken structures began to move. From every crevice, hideaway, door and window, people emerged. Their boot steps crunched through debris. They wore dirty vinyl, torn paper, and furs that were smudged and burnt. Both male and female, some had cascades of hair: midnight, tawny, orange. Others had none at all.

The street people quickly surrounded Sarine and her companions, pale hands, dark hands holding weapons of every sort from scorebeams to sticks. They weren't wraiths, but real; the city was only dead in disguise. Sarine felt her knife pressing against her calf, the heaviness of her scorebeam in her pack. Both were useless now. She heard Sterling rustle, saw him take a defensive stance. It wouldn't save them.

"Hold, Sterling," she said quietly.

The robot relaxed and straightened. Time unfroze. Everything breathed again. Up ahead, a torn piece of canvas flapped like a ghost in the breeze. The energy of the surrounding gang foretold violence.

"We don't have much." Grath fingered his pack straps. He seemed quite at ease. His lack of fear gave him a calm Sarine craved. She only hoped that fearlessness wouldn't lead to reckless moves. She was still afraid.

"You can have mine," Grath said, his pack now sliding off his arms.

"We're not thieves." The same voice they'd heard before spoke again. It belonged to a small man, bald and with

30

skin so red it looked flayed. Half his face was formed wrong. The cheek looked swollen with tumor. The edge of his mouth, slit up too far, formed a perpetual grimace. But the eyes shone twilight blue, bright as beads, and Sarine met them unflinching.

"You tell 'em, Ugly," someone from the crowd said.

A woman, head shaved, her face covered with abstract tattoos, muttered, "Is it because of how we look that you think us thieves? We like the way we look. What about Silver there?" She gestured rudely at Sterling. "He's not even human."

Sarine did not answer. Grath hung onto his pack with his right hand. It swung slowly back and forth, making a brown shadow on the pavement. Ash and dust skittered around them in the eddying wind. Beyond, the hills and tower brightened, but the light didn't seem to touch the city's bleak air.

The man called Ugly took several steps toward them. He was not armed, but he looked terrifying. Sarine had seen worse on the Edge. Deformities were rare, but they occurred more in gang babies than anywhere else. She held very still.

"The guard job, eh?" Ugly said.

"Yes."

Suddenly, he came at her. It was too quick. She had little time to think as, hands raised, the man leapt for her midsection. She stepped to one side, caught him lightly and flung him over her shoulder. He landed with a thick grunt behind her. The crowd laughed.

"I'm sorry," she said, looking down.

He got up, brushing his worn, dull vinyl and said, "That was good."

"Ugly, dammit!" said a new voice.

Ugly looked up at the same time Sarine did. A man came forward, chin-length chestnut hair, golden face that looked too smooth to be real. His tall form was slim beneath black vinyl trousers, broad-shouldered under a layer of fairly clean synth fur.

"Are you all right?" he asked the smaller man.

"Sure," Ugly said.

"It's not your job to test them," he said. "You're going to get killed one day, proving the Magistrate wrong in not choosing you."

Ugly lobbed him once in the shoulder with his fist. "You don't think I can fight? You don't think I can defend myself?"

"I didn't say that."

"Who else is going to test them?" Ugly asked. "You?"

"Hey, Beautiful," someone called, "you wouldn't want to get your hands dirty."

The man turned, his hand coming up fisted with the first and ring fingers extended. The common, rude hand signal could mean many things, all of them offensive.

"Who are you people?" Sarine asked.

"Perimeter lookout," Ugly said.

"Means we couldn't make the cut as real guards," Beautiful added.

"But you're still employed?" Grath asked.

"So they call it. We get food and other necessities, but little else," Ugly said. "Some of us moonlight in other things, too." He squinted, wrinkled, lop-sided face eyeing them askance.

"Why do you stay?" Sterling asked.

"We all have different reasons." Beautiful touched Ugly's shoulder with the flat of his palm, standing a half-step behind him. Light seemed to fuse with his skin, making it glow. "We'll take you to the Magistrate," he said. "That's where you apply for the job. It's a joke, though. The tower doesn't need protection. The army within it can zap anything they sense coming their way." He smiled, lips parting. The perfect teeth glistened like pearls. His voice held a natural, musical cadence.

"The guard's a formality," Ugly put in. "To keep the tourists out, mostly." His own yellow teeth were impossibly crooked, and his voice came out pinched. He was still angry. "But it's a job. We'll take you only if you hire us as deputies if you get the position."

"Sounds fair," Grath said.

Sarine glared at him.

"What else are you going to do?" he asked, raising both hands in a shrug.

"All right," she finally agreed, though she had no intention of making it a promise.

When they realized there'd be no more dramatics, the crowd began to disperse. Sarine's agreement seemed to satisfy Beautiful and Ugly, and they led them to the end of the street, then up a stained alley where they stepped carefully to avoid an avenue of broken glass.

"Beautiful here's a half-path," Ugly said as they walked. "If you get the job, having us as your deputies will make you strong. He may not be army material—he's not full-blown—but his talent's still valuable."

"What's a half-path?" Sarine asked.

"Telepath." Ugly scratched at his enlarged, red cheek, then ogled Beautiful, craning his neck. "A full-path can read your thoughts. He reads emotions, though. Desires."

"Make good money at it, too, on the carnival side," Beautiful added.

"Reading desires?" Grath said, turning around to look at Beautiful.

"And fulfilling them," Beautiful replied, eyebrows rising to dare him to challenge. Grath quickly looked down.

Ugly laughed, rolling his twilight blue eyes.

Sarine had no doubt he was telling the truth. People always paid to obtain beauty in all its guises. She wondered, though, where Ugly fit in. Grath had backed away a step, as though offended.

Hey, you did what you had to do. Her nose pricked with tears as she thought of her family she'd left behind and especially Tyranny. Beautiful's clear, brown eyes were like her son's. She would have let him come with her, but his ties to the others were strong, as they should be. Her own mother had left her when she was a baby. Later, in his teens, Tyranny would probably father children whom he'd later leave. Adulthood was a new road that did not often include the very young. The gang-family was nurturer and provider, not a single mother, or father. You outgrew it in time.

Beautiful came alongside Sarine as they stopped at a sealed, metal door. Voice low, he said, "Don't be nervous." A half-smile embedded into her mind sending a soft, more private signal: *The grief will pass.*

Surprised, she actually blushed. She knew they weren't lying about his talent, but she'd never felt a telepath's thoughts before. Like a wind through her soul.

Beautiful's long-fingered hand found a hidden button on the frame and the door slid open to a stale-smelling passageway that rode a slight incline into deeper shadow.

They all followed Beautiful into the hall. Worn, flat carpet rotted beneath their feet, the dim pattern forming swirls of dark edging dark. At the end of the hall, another door opened revealing brilliant light, a room full of greens, and fresh spring scent.

"Green Forever," Sterling said softly. "Captured."

Plants of all kinds sprouted from above them, beside them, at their feet. Some had feathered fronds; others were ropey and coiled like verdant snakes, air-bathing. Ivy crawled over tree trunks and up distant, curved walls. Thick grass carpeted the floor, giving way to a curving, stone path. Something rang softly like bells and a breeze followed it, rifling Sarine's long hair with the tart perfume of lilies. Above the indoor jungle she saw a curved roof, plasti-glass or something stronger, and walls in hexagonal shapes that rounded into the dome structure.

"I wouldn't have guessed this would be here in the middle of this city," Sarine said.

"The Magistrate keeps it this way. She lives here part of the time. Robots tend it." Ugly gestured toward an overgrown fern where beneath it a four-legged robot carefully trimmed away all the brown fronds with one pincer. The robot was painted green to blend in with the scenery. Sterling stepped toward it, fascinated.

Further off to the other side, another robot, bronze and more human-shaped, gathered dead leaves into a shiny, green sack. The air was damp. The light bell-sound came again, making Sarine's spine tingle.

"Is the Magistrate here now?" Sarine asked.

"No, but she will be," Ugly said, moving ahead of them on the path. "Our entrance alerted her. Either she'll come, or send one of her assistants to find out why we're here."

Grath went off the path to touch the rough bark of a small tree, the trunk a darker shade of brown against his hand. The dome seemed spacious, roomy, but it wasn't much bigger than the span of half the building itself—maybe a hundred feet wide. The height gave it an extended feel.

Without warning, a woman appeared on the path before them. Sarine froze. Sterling went rigid beside the four-legged trimmer, one foot forward, arms up and bent in the defensive stance he took when sparring with Sarine. Grath merely glanced over from the tree, calm as always. Ugly and Beautiful stood up straight.

"Hologram," Sarine hissed at Sterling, her own heart still tumbling through its routine from the surprise.

"Of course." Sterling relaxed slightly. "My eyes can discern hologram from reality quite well."

Sarine bit her lip to keep from smiling at Sterling's attempt to deny his first, panicked reaction.

"Zeth," the image of the woman said to Ugly, "what are you doing? Bringing me strangers again? I have no need of anyone right now." She was a small woman with short black hair and a mouth almost as wide as her face. She turned to dismiss him.

"The position of the guard, Magistrate Nola, is not yet filled."

"The head guard? Who's applying?" She turned back, glancing from Sterling to Grath, completely overlooking Sarine.

"I am." Sarine stepped forward.

When Sarine finished giving her qualifications, Magistrate Nola said, "Impressive but you're a little young. Can you read?"

Sarine shook her head.

"She can learn." Sterling stepped forward.

"No." Nola turned away. She wore thin vinyl slacks, a vinyl bra. Her musculature was small, lean. Her skin looked like faked gold pigment. "I don't think we can use you."

"Wait." Sarine went toward her. "Has anyone else applied? Could I try a temporary position?"

Nola crossed her arms over her chest. "I'm sure you are a good fighter, but the job requires administrative and leadership duties as well."

Out the corner of her eye, Sarine saw Grath slouched against the tree trunk, that inner calm of his making him appear almost lazy, without expectation. She remembered his view: "You create your own future. Your own reality. Everything is connected. There is no end." Breathlessly, she said, "Give me a job to do, an assignment. Anything. I'll tend your plants. I'll sweep the streets. I'll learn to read. Then you can assess my performance. I'd like to get to know this city better anyway." It felt heavy with secrets. She liked that.

Nola stared at her, arms still tightly crossed, lips pursed. "That's the first time anyone's offered to sweep the streets," she said, chuckling. "The only thing I can come up with is a mystery no one's been able to solve in six months. The EM fields of the city have been requiring daily manual adjustments to keep the Walled City from disrupting them.

36

Normally, no adjustments are needed. Someone has invaded us with a disruptor device. It could be anywhere, disguised as anything. Find it and I guarantee the job to be yours."

Sarine felt her breath leave her, her emotions cave in to flat disappointment. The Magistrate described a near-impossible task. She tried not to show her frustration. "I'll do it." Her voice came out dry, hard.

"Fine." Nola fingered an elaborate bio-pacer on her left wrist. It was jeweled, and flashed in light from a source they could not see. "I'll meet you back here in a week and see what you've come up with. That's the best I can do; I'm sorry." But she did not sound sorry.

"I will," Sarine said, glancing down. The path beneath her feet was porous and flaking. She kicked at a shard of cement.

"Oh, and one more thing," Nola said, starting to walk away.

"What?"

"Learn to read." Her form vanished like a light being shut off.

Sarine pressed her fists to her hips. At least she'd gotten a chance.

*

"We'll help you," Ugly said. "We know this city upside-down."

Beautiful nodded in agreement.

Sarine stared at their single room, a home not nearly as nice as her cramped bubble, with a sagging double bed, no kitchen, no bathroom, and walls that were bare plaster. At least their sink had running water for washing. Though she'd known the nomad life all her years, and was used to roughing it, she was still appalled at their living conditions. No heat. Rags for clothes. Quick-pac food cooked over a solar-battery powered hot-plate. The gangs, at least, had had fields and gardens, had harvested wild as well as domestic fruits and vegetables. They stole what they couldn't make, and lived quite well.

Beautiful and Ugly's greatest luxuries were a supply of stim-wafers and two hemi-synchs. Escapist entertainment in the form of drugs mixed with the hemi-synch headset didn't come cheap. They could've had a real apartment or home for what they'd paid for those devices, and were still probably paying for them, any capital they earned no doubt taken off their credit accrual before they ever saw it. A hemi-synch could keep you broke if you weren't rich. Only the gangs avoided the credit system everyone seemed to belong to, since they didn't barter with money.

For now, Sarine and Sterling chose to sleep in their bubble in the little side yard just outside Ugly and Beautiful's ground-floor room. The Magistrate of Moltenrose had offered no facilities and Sarine had not asked. Grath had gone off to explore, and they hadn't seen him since.

Afternoon light filtered through the window and ignited the dust so the air glittered. Beautiful sat in the midst of it, haloed, angelic. Ugly stayed in shadow, demon-mated, and it was still hard for Sarine to imagine them as lovers. They looked so unsuited to each other, but then, she supposed, so did she and Sterling.

The floor, splintering hardwood, was uncomfortable for her, and she leaned part of her weight against the coldness of Sterling as the four of them discussed, again and again, the technology of disruptors, what they might look like, their weaknesses, their limits. Before Grath had left, he'd loaned Sarine his library. Sterling, silver limbs spattered with the reflected rusts of the room, accessed research information and read it aloud to her.

"It'll be impossible to find it," Ugly kept saying. His hand trailed over the frayed laces of his boots. "If the technology is so perfected, it could be anywhere."

38

"The size of a pebble," Beautiful added, nodding in a bronze haze of back-lit motes. His gold-dark hair took on a shimmering glaze. "It could be inside another device, disguised as a hemi-synch, or a piece of jewelry, a bio-pacer."

"It could be implanted inside a person," Ugly glanced at Sterling, waiting.

Sarine watched the red eyes come up, focus on the others, then her. "It's true," he said. "There is no indication the disruptor has to be stationary to operate. Its limits are distance and the fact that the electro-magnetic fields here are being manually adjusted every day or so to compensate for it. It is not doing so much damage, but it is a nuisance."

"How far from the generator before it stops working?" Sarine asked. "That would narrow our search perimeter."

"Ten miles in any direction."

"It could be outside the city, then," Ugly said.

"Would anything block it?" she asked.

"Only distance. And our bio-pacers disrupt its frequency. It is as if its purpose isn't to harm us, but to create a hole in the fields themselves. But for what purpose?" Sterling held the library in one hand, not looking at its mini-screen.

"A hole?" Beautiful leaned back on his hands, palms flat, fingers splayed. His lips shone with a faint patina of saliva. "What other reason do you make a hole unless it's to let something in."

"Or take something out," Ugly finished.

"Well, anything can get in or out of Moltenrose. The EM fields protect us from the Walled City's mind control. That's it. Along with our bio-pacers," Sarine speculated.

"Then what might be trying to get in—our out--," Beautiful said, "is either non-corporeal…"

"…or," Ugly interrupted, "something that operates within a different set of fields that make ours poison to it."

They all turned to Sterling.

"A machine, perhaps, but not one like myself," he said. "I am not affected by field densities. They are directed at your brains, specifically the acetacholine manufacture. I don't have that chemical within me. Whatever wants to come in or out through this 'hole' must be yet another type of machine, or life different from my own and from yours."

"Is there anything like that in your memory?" Sarine asked Sterling. Despite the wipe of his life experience and creation memories, Sterling was a warehouse of trivia.

"The spychiatrist," he replied calmly.

"Shit!" Beautiful sat up, jamming his fists together, the whites of his eyes seeming to pop with brilliance.

Ugly simply let out his breath in a long whoosh.

"I've seen one of those once," Beautiful exclaimed. "They're horrible." He came up onto his knees. "They can't come here, supposedly. Can't pass through our psychic shields. But if one could...shit. Oh shit." He closed his eyes tightly. "They have arms like an octopus, retractable syringes on the ends. They're the ultimate puppeteers. Robot-things with drugs and wave emissions that can control your mind with one shot."

"These are the things Grath said could travel time," Sarine commented to Sterling.

"I don't know what they are, if they're alive or not." Beautiful continued, rubbing hard at his forehead. "I saw a holo on them once. One spychiatrist controlled a whole group of people all at once. It made them hurt themselves and others. It can make you believe anything. Like a hemi-synch gone wild. The holo showed a guy masturbating under their control until he had ripped himself to shreds. It can cause personality changes in a second, like a total reprogramming. It can give pain or pleasure with a single directed beam. It alters your brain."

"If they're alive, they have no conscience," Ugly said.

"Gave me nightmares for months." Beautiful chewed on his thumbnail.

"Grath mentioned them to me," Sarine said. "I hadn't heard of them before."

40

"They're myths, it seems. This library of his has no information on them I can access," Sterling reported.

"Oh they're very real," Beautiful said.

"We need to find Grath. Maybe he knows something else that can help us." Sarine started to stand.

"If all this is true," Ugly said, rising to his feet and waddling to the shelf above the double bed, "I need a stim." There was a dirty, glass jar there that held multi-colored plastic wafers. He grabbed a green one with his fat fingers and broke it open. The essence sparked up at his face like mini-lightning. It struck him with a tiny pop on his upper lip where it glowed orange for a moment, then faded. Ugly grinned, his body visibly relaxing.

"Bring me one while you're at it," Beautiful called over his shoulder. Then he lowered his head into his hands, combing long fingers through shiny, chin-length hair and mumbled, "Make it two."

*

The last person to see Grath was a girl no more than sixteen. She sat hunched in rags in the filthy door front of a tilted building where a temporary, traveling XXX holo-show had set up. Tattooed, black filigree detailing tiny vines and roses outlined her lips. Just above the bridge of her nose a tattoo of an insect body left her eyebrows looking like wings.

"They're gonna give me a job in there. I'm just waitin' for the owner," she said, voice hoarse as if she were recovering from a cold. "I saw you guys come into town. The dark-haired one with you went off with Tana. It was late last night."

"We know her," Ugly said. "Thanks." He patted her on the head. Her dun hair was filled with braids that looked more tangled than ordered. At the little parts, Sarine could see the scalp was peeling.

"Good luck with that job," Sarine said.

The girl nodded but did not smile.

The sky was slate. More rain patterned their path. The street, where it wasn't crumbling, grew slippery. Beautiful complained about it long and loud. "I hate getting wet! This rain's pure shit." He slicked his damp hair back with his fingers and glowered.

"You won't die from it," Ugly muttered.

Sterling endured it silently, though Sarine knew he probably hated it as much as Beautiful. The raindrops stuck to his metal body like glue, and dried in spots resembling scales. Grooming was important to Sterling in his own way, and rain inconvenienced him as much as it did humans caught out in the downpour.

Tana's rooms were empty when they got there, fresh trash littering the floors: empty food cans, broken stim wafers. They found a single, gold loop earring in the pile, the clasp broken. "She moved," Ugly said, kicking a food tin with the scuffed toe of his boot.

"Looks recent," Sarine observed.

"Maybe she got a job on the carny side," Beautiful suggested. "Anyway, we can ask around. She'll show up. She always does."

"I just want to get to Grath," Sarine said. "I know he can help us." It wasn't only Grath's roadside philosophy that had impressed Sarine. He was smart. If anyone could figure out the 'hows' and 'whys' of the disruptor, he could.

They spent the rest of the afternoon asking around, but no one could help them.

That night, she shared food with Beautiful and Ugly, then left them basking on their bed as she went outside to their small weedy yard choked with rain-damp grime, and her bubble. In his delicate, yet masculine voice, Sterling asked, "Would you like to spar?"

Sarine shook her head.

"You seem preoccupied."

42

In truth, she was. Sterling read her moods well. She'd been thinking, since they'd met that girl with the peeling scalp, about the relationships of things, about reality and what you made of it, about truth as seen from different views. There were other times, other dimensions. An unlimited scope to the universe, what it was, what it meant, what it could be. And yet, girls like her friend Marri died shrieking in denial, or ended up on the steps of a sex show begging for work. Sarine herself had regrets. When she'd found Sterling she'd been a murderer, a thief, a sister, a mother. She hadn't really thought much about living as an adult apart from the Wolf-Spiders.

How quickly, now, she'd entered into this new view of the world, this new existence. She missed Tyranny's young wonder and devilish curiosity, and yet, things were fresh and interesting for her without him. The new Sarine cared, as she had not in the gang, about far-off things, things she couldn't see and that might not affect her this instant. Her vision had widened. She liked that. And with this unusual aptitude toward empathy, she thought she might like to find that young girl again, clean her up and deputize her. That was, of course, if she managed the impossible and found the disruptor.

"I need the job," she said, turning to Sterling who, with the patience born only of machines, stood silent and ready always at her side. "We've got to find Grath."

"Tomorrow we'll start early and look harder." The red eyes in the dark looked like animal eyes.

She nodded, taking his hand. The gentle moans of their friends' lovemaking drifted out the window. "Let's go in the bubble and talk about this," Sarine said, pulling him away from the outside wall.

Inside the bubble, all environmental noise was filtered out. She could hear the quiet shush of her own breathing, and Sterling's faint machine sigh. *He has a heart,* she thought, *like a rumble of thunder caught and distilled to a purr.*

"Do you want to talk?" Sterling asked, settling on the bed. He removed one shoulder plate and rubbed at the water stains with his hard fingertips. The scraping sound etched the air.

As she looked at his human-form face, her own features distorted in its mirror, and as her gaze met the red lights behind the darkened, clearsteel of his sculpted human-shaped eyes, she realized she had no words. She slid out of her bulky clothing and knelt beside him on the bed, her long hair furrowing forward, dusky white against her breasts. "I should make you give me a reading lesson."

"We have time for that later," Sterling replied, dropping the carapace and reaching up to cup her face. His hands felt glossy and cold, but she didn't mind.

*

"Your ornament for rent?" inquired a stocky man, young, with green hair. He appeared to have no lips.

Sarine gazed through a haze of incense, smoke and parti-colored streamers into the tattoo bar. "What?"

Beyond their host a large room was filled with people, some laughing, some talking, some having needles stuck into various body parts for the seeming popular art of tattoo carving.

"Him." The man gestured toward Sterling. "Your robot. Do you sell his time?"

Sarine blinked, caught off-guard. "No." She almost snarled, then caught herself. "Hey, no offense. We're just looking for someone. Maybe you know her. Tana?"

"Know her. Don't know where she went, though." He swept his green hair back with a scarred hand. Abstract tattoos marred the skin that wasn't bubbled from past injury.

"Do you know where she lives?" Sarine asked.

"Not me, but maybe someone here. Come in. Buy a tattoo, a stim or a smoke. You have credit, don't you?"

Sarine shook her head.

The man scowled. Beyond the smoke, a young man giggled, then groaned as needles touched his naked thighs. Two other people were making love standing up in a corner. The large room smelled of ash and spice.

Hesitant, Sarine said, "Can you tell me who might know?"

The man shrugged. "Surly in the corner there." He pointed to the couple undulating against each other. "But he's preoccupied, I guess." He grinned, showing a missing front tooth, the rest long and very yellow.

"I'll wait." Sarine looked around for a place to sit, out of the way but not hidden. She saw a sprung couch by a wall and went to it. Sterling sat beside her, his red gaze scanning the room back and forth. "Interesting, huh?" The people were not like her own friends from her gang…they seemed even wilder, more self-destructive. And yet, there was a kind of family bond among them. They shared the commonality of their art.

"Yes," he replied.

A woman, older than Sarine, quite suddenly sat down beside her. "Howdy to you and your friend. New?"

Sarine nodded.

"Ever get tattooed? It's the greatest. You should, you know." Her short hair, nut-brown and separated into a million curls gave her a soft look, but her eyes were hard chips of blue that made her look older inside than out.

"Doesn't it hurt?" Sarine asked.

"Every tattoo I've ever gotten has hurt. But it's a cleansing. You have to do it to understand. It's like ridding yourself of this world and glimpsing the next. If divinity can be found in a little bit of pain, what's the harm?"

Sarine shrugged. More religion? Touching other worlds through art? Not as easily done as thought, she was sure. "Do you know Tana?"

"Tana? Sure. She's one of the queens, devoted to the art. Beautiful. If I could have her courage…"

"Do you know where she lives? She's an old friend. I can't seem to catch up to her."

"Oh, sure." Her hands were untouched, though her arms contained snakes and roses and toothy fish. One silver ring glittered on her middle finger, which she pointed haphazardly in the air. "Know the wall with the motto?" She paused, then said, "You know, the painted mural: 'What's It Worth?'"

Sarine nodded, though she didn't know. But surely Beautiful and Ugly would.

"Go right at that wall, down a quarter of a block, then down the cement staircase. She moved in the basement there a few days ago. Said she wanted more privacy than her old place gave her. Haven't seen her since she moved, though."

"Hey, thanks." Sarine sat forward. "Sterling, we gotta go."

The woman eyed Sterling with lethargic interest, then jumped up and scurried across the room to join a group watching art come to life on a woman's bared breast. As soon as she turned away, she seemed to forget them entirely. In the other corner, Surly was still pressed against his lover, an indistinct shadow with ringed hands that gripped the sides of his torn, vinyl jacket. The man with green hair had moved into a group in the center, animatedly talking, his hands waving through the air.

"Let's go," she said to her robot.

Sarine and Sterling walked outside into clouded noon sun. Sidewalks crumbled beneath them, and buildings sagged on the other side of the street.

"Let's find Ugly and Beautiful," Sarine said.

Sterling nodded.

Sarine's eyes stung from the smoke, the fresher air making them water. She realized as she walked beside Sterling toward Ugly and Beautiful's apartment how

46

unprepared she'd been for the harshness and indifference of city dwellers who seemed to belong to no one but the streets. Where did they fit in Grath's impressive plan? Were they as afraid as she was of dying? Of living?

"Do you ever wonder where you came from?" she asked Sterling,

"Yes. But more than that, I wonder where we all came from. I have a creator, of course, as do you in the form of a parent. We all do, or we wouldn't be here. But someone or something else created them."

"Your questions aren't that different from mine, then," she said.

"Why should they be?"

Sarine smiled, held out her hand to him. "I agree."

The street ahead of them fed on dust and age. In different times, it led to different places.

"There are no limits," Grath had said.

But at the moment, she felt very unconnected and limited in her life. Everything was still too new. Only Sterling remained familiar. But at this point, even that relationship seemed limited to her. If the ability for mind control won out against the world's defenses against the Walled City, living would become even more limited, yet ignorance would keep them from knowing or wanting more. Was there a point in existing at all if desire and freedom were taken? If awareness of a person's own limits was curbed, it might be a blessing. With awareness, Sarine could only see limitation as an enemy.

Sarine had to find this disruptor, if for no other reason than her own personal peace. The job would be only one benefit.

*

"Hey, there's day, finally," Sterling observed, out of sync with the rest of them, as was common. Sarine looked up, the weather the last thing on her mind as they walked toward Tana's.

Beautiful and Ugly were struck equally by the slanting rays of the afternoon sun pushing out from behind a rip in the cloud cover. Beautiful looked shiny and new, almost as glossy as Sterling, though his eyebrows were narrowed as if some dark mood preoccupied him. Sarine figured it wasn't easy being a telepath, or half-path, even with only haphazard abilities.

Ugly's ruddiness turned sallow in the sudden light, and the bone ridges and scars on his reddened scalp became more visible. He looked like he was frowning as he waved 'hello' to a man and woman smoking hand-rolled cigarettes on the corner, his face merely a mask wrongly depicting the character within. He walked with a jolt in each step, hyperactively ready for any encounter they might make.

Sarine recognized in Ugly a countenance of survival instinct. He probably would not have survived the injuries to his face and head otherwise. Good medical care never left scars these days, if you could get it. Gangs suffered, too, letting the injured die on the Edge, using only the border clinics in rare cases.

Sarine projected out with her mind, trying to predict the future for now. Impossible, she knew. But what was the flow? The events caught in her path, on the Green Forever wind. Surely deep logic would help in this situation, if not supernatural talent. Nature formed the current. She had only to tap it. Grath's philosophy made sense there.

The gravel alley ended in dirt. On the wall facing them a huge mural, spackled with sand-weathering and water stains, still showed a vast spacescape, stars like eyes and silvery ships with gunwales pointed at a ruined landscape. A blackened skeleton of a city crawled forward on the horizon. The design seemed to communicate overkill. The words **What's It Worth** were painted in red over the scene. Her lessons were working. She could actually read them.

They walked along the length of the wall, the ships seeming to move along with them.

"Who painted it?" Sarine asked.

Ugly tipped one shoulder in a half-shrug. "Don't know. It's been there since I can remember."

"It was done when the city was still alive," Beautiful said. "By someone with hooks for hands. At least that's what rumor says. But I can't believe it. I wouldn't think it would hold up this well if it was that old."

They found the steps going down. At the bottom, a locked metal door blocked them.

Ugly pounded on it with his fist. The knocking echoed back to them from somewhere far inside. Ugly turned, unsure, rubbing sore knuckles with his thumbs, then his lips. "Nobody home perhaps?"

"Try again," Sarine said quietly.

Sterling moved to obey, his knuckles clanging against it with sharp explosions. Sarine thought she even saw sparks.

After a long minute, Sterling poised to try again when a muffled voice within shouted, "Who?"

"Tana? It's Ugly. Haven't seen you around."

"Go away!"

"Just want to talk," Ugly said loudly. "Open. Come on."

The door inched open. Brown eyes blinked out from the crack. A silver ring in the left nostril of a long, straight nose caught the dim, outside light like a trembling tear. "What are you doing here? What do you want?"

"I'm looking for my friend Grath," Sarine said, stepping forward.

"Oh." The door started to close. "Don't know him. Haven't seen him."

Sterling took the initiative to place a foot in the door. As Tana tried to close it, it jammed. "You were seen with him," Sterling said.

"Robot-man, get your foot outta my door!" Her voice was breathless suddenly, filled with guilt.

"She's lying," Beautiful announced.

Sarine didn't have to be a half-path to guess that herself. She leaned toward the crack. "Grath?" she called. "Are you all right? Grath?"

"Get away!" Tana screamed. She kicked at Sterling's foot, hopped back and groaned. Ugly flung the door open and they all entered. A long hall led to a distant rectangle of light. The lights on the ceiling were half burnt out, making the hall obscure, twi-lit.

"You have no right," the bald, illustrated girl said again and again as they passed her. Her hands were fists, glittering with chains and rings. She wore no more than a simple, vinyl shift, sleeveless, legless.

"What's going on?" shouted a voice from the rectangle of light. A silhouette appeared there. The rectangle became a doorway into a large, bright room. The silhouette became dark Grath, braid caught in his hand as he stepped forward.

"What are you all doing here?" Grath asked. His smile did not reveal teeth. His eyes looked bloodshot, red-rimmed.

"Grath," Sarine said, coming forward until they stood face to face. She was relieved to see he was, other than tired, all right. The way Tana reacted, she harbored a dead body. "We've been looking for you. We were hoping you could help us with the technology to locate the disrupt..." She stopped, her eyes catching the movement of something silvery flashing in the room behind Grath. "What's that?" She tried to go around him, but Grath reached up suddenly, palm to her shoulder pushing hard. Instinct and training took over and she lithely stepped aside, letting his own weight propel him forward, past her, falling with a crack to his knees. Now, her view into the big room unblocked, she saw what moved. What sparkled. What Tana and Grath had been hiding.

The machine had five, many-jointed arms with crab-claw hands that clasped and unclasped as if to catch the air. Its

50

fat, round body, the center for the arms and, apparently, its brain, glittered as a series of lights chased themselves across the surface, round and round. Gold light, cerise and lime. It hovered without outward means of propellant. It made a soft whirring sound, not unlike Sterling when she listened to him breathe. As she stared at it, it rotated, pointing one of its long arms toward her as if to beckon.

Her spine went cold. "You…" But the accusation came out a whisper, weak, unsure.

"Don't go in there!" Grath shouted.

In the background, Tana still screamed. "You have no right! You have no right!"

Sarine glanced to her left. Sterling had come up alongside her, Beautiful and Ugly flanking him a half-step behind.

"It will kill you," Grath shouted, slowly rising, using the wall for support. "Only Tana knows how…"

Ugly turned sharply and kicked Grath in the chest with the toe of his boot. Grath sat back hard, glaring. "How dare you?" Ugly hissed. "Where's that disruptor?"

Tana tried to run by them, but Beautiful grabbed her arm, flinging her against the wall. "So you were the spy. Did the Walled City send you? Did you have the disruptor all along?"

"I'm not a spy," she insisted. "I made the disruptor to steal the spychiatrist."

"Idiot! It can destroy us all!"

Inside the room, Sarine saw the machine star to move toward them.

"That's a spychiatrist? It's moving!" Sarine backed up, nearly tripping over Beautiful. "Make it stop."

At once, Tana stopped resisting in Beautiful's arms. "Only if you leave."

"You do control it, then," Sarine stated, glancing back to see the machine continue its advance.

"Yes."

51

"She has the disruptor," Grath said. "But you don't understand. Sarine. Sarine. This is our chance. The spychiatrist can open doors if we can control it, keep it deaf to enemy commands. Tana wants the same thing. She's not a spy."

"It's controlled from the Walled City! You let it in knowing that!" Ugly yelled, accusing Grath.

"I did!" Tana shouted back, sticking out her chin. Her bald head seemed to glow, the tattoos on it like a map of blue veins snaking its net about her scalp.

"It knows she has the disruptor. It knows it can only survive if it obeys her. She's the only thing that can keep it from succumbing to Moltenrose's EM fields." Again, Grath tried to stand. "Don't you see? It obeys her! She's stolen it right out from under their noses. We can control it."

"Where is the disruptor?" Sarine asked Tana, stepping back further as the machine slowly kept coming. It was only a few feet away from the door now.

"I won't tell you! You can't destroy it. It's worth a fortune!"

"You will tell me!" Beautiful demanded, his perfect face marred by the tightening of his eyes and mouth as he concentrated. "Ah... Your mind is too easy." He reached up toward her face, his open hand grasping, then freezing as a blue cloud from the spychiatrist, now hovering just inside the doorway, bathed them all in its sudden light.

Sarine felt instant paralytic euphoria. Her insides swam like smoke, and her view swirled, a pinpoint now, though still complete. Somehow, the essence of the Edge, her son Tyranny, and her friends closed in on her. She longed for them, could almost smell wild fennel and the locust trees that bordered their territory. If she just turned her mind inward, she could go back. And yet, there was Sterling to consider.

She stared, the pinpoint view widening a little, and concentrated on the outside world, the motionless bodies of her friends, the spychiatrist as it hummed over their heads, silver arms poised, spider-like. She couldn't blink, and her eyes hazed over, but still she watched.

A bright beam of light shot out from its underside, carving a bloody gash across Tana's frozen face. Her forehead and nose split open to the bone. Dark blood spurted. The ring in Tana's nose fell to the floor, a red-drenched metal jewel.

At first Sarine thought it was all a trick of light. Time seemed stopped. In that non-instant, nothing could happen. Nothing was. Then she realized she'd just witnessed a murder. A machine had just murdered a human being. Tana had controlled nothing in the end.

Fresh blood gushed over what remained of Tana's cheeks and chin. The skin of her scalp, where it wasn't lined by tattoos, looked blue-white.

And Sarine remembered Marri. Remembered the denial of death. And struggled, trying to form the word 'no' through the blue fog of her consciousness. But it was as if ice held her. Or heavy earth. She couldn't move a muscle, and wondered if even her heart had somehow frozen in this non-moment, this envelope outside time.

Then, so quick she could barely comprehend it, Sterling hurled through the air to land on top of Tana, his silver fingers brushing the floor where the nose-ring/disruptor lay, crushing it beneath his hard, metal palm.

Suddenly, Sarine was free. The blue cloud vanished and the spychiatrist whined, a wrenching scream that drilled into her ears and chest. She saw Grath grab at his ears. Beautiful and Ugly leaned like sleepwalkers against the wall. And beneath the spychiatrist, Sterling slipped forward against slick blood, still grasping the crushed nose-ring in his left hand.

The machine's death scream rose in pitch, and Sarine saw a white beam lash out toward Sterling, heard a loud pop, tasted burning metal.

Something crashed to her right. When she could see again, the spychiatrist lay on the floor, arms dangling, one arm crushed beneath its bulk. Beside it, a blackened Sterling reclined on his side, face turned at an awkward angle as if to look up, eyes dark, blank, dead.

Sarine saw time spin out and away again, all the doors Grath had promised in his eternal hologram closing with final, strategic booms.

*

In the arboretum of the Magistrate, the glass ceiling and the bright leaves threw sunset back on itself, giving the room a brown and maroon soft-focus appearance. Sarine smelled jasmine distance, and something burnt and spicy on the edges of her tongue. With dream-like sense, she saw how the day affected the room, how Beautiful looked sculpted from darkest gold, how Grath had changed from affectionate stranger to brooding shadow. How even Ugly, as he had helped lug first Sterling and then the broken spychicatrist back to the Magistrate's office, seemed less horrific.

She had the job. The Magistrate kept her promise. But for Sarine it was little compensation as she watched the robot doctors and visiting specialists, most arriving via hologram, assess the situation. Sterling lay bent and broken in a little room overlooking the indoor garden. His body, once brilliant, alive with reflections, had turned black. Even acid baths couldn't remove all the soot without damaging his exterior, and so he lay, vulnerable to the whims of cyber experts, no better than dead to Sarine.

"A robot can't die," Beautiful said by her side.

"They'll repair him good as new," Ugly added.

Grath said nothing, went to wander through the orchards, still looking, perhaps, for his hidden doors. Sarine couldn't care about that right now, couldn't even care enough to yell at him, though anger drenched her, and grief.

"He was more than just a robot," Sarine said.

"Give it time." And Ugly patted her wrist with his knobby fingers, the hair from his knuckles brushing her skin like fur.

When the stars came out overhead, the glass looked pitted with them; automatic sprinklers buzzed on. The beads of water made their own constellations in the grass as Sarine walked over it toward the little room. It had been hours since Sterling's 'death' and still no word. She could see movement beyond the room's windows. The cyber experts still worked, still conferred over her lover, over the toy-droid whose favorite season was Green Forever.

She stopped at the door wanting to go inside, wanting to be with him, yet felt stupid in her actions. Would they laugh at her? He's just a machine, her mind told her. Only little girls cry over broken dolls.

She knocked. The door opened and a less sophisticated robot with blue eye-lights and a hole for a mouth, droned, "Come in. We have made some progress."

Her heart jolted in her chest. "Progress?"

"Repairs are on-going. But there is no knowledge yet if his memory banks remain intact, or whatever personality he had incorporated during his up-time."

"I understand. I just wanted to see…"

"Of course." The robot didn't hesitate, just motioned her on toward the bed where another robot tech worked on a keyboard attached to Sterling's blackened head. He looked less twisted, lying there, as if someone had come along and straightened out his limbs, made him more comfortable. His eyes stared, still lightless, but his lips were parted as though he breathed. Sarine listened for the familiar whirring sound, the purr of his robot heart. Heard nothing.

Throat tight, she went to his side.

"You can touch him," the robot said.

She frowned at the strange statement. "Why? How could it matter?"

"It matters to you, does it not?" it asked.

"Yes."

"Then you should, of course, touch him."

The fact that it referred to Sterling as 'him' told her this robot saw the model on the pallet as superior, more human than itself at the very least. For some reason, that made a difference to her, and she reached out to take Sterling's cold hand in her own. The chill felt familiar, good. She hadn't expected otherwise, but somewhere a little warmth touched off inside her. Sterling wasn't human. He couldn't really die. He had a chance to come back to her. A chance Marri never had.

Holding his sooty hand, Sarine stared straight at the damp garden through the window, at nature caught and held in a small, indoor cage, yet thriving, not knowing it was separate from the whole seasonal pattern. Not caring if it was reading fake signals from a world within a world. All that mattered was that it was alive. And growing.

As Sterling had been.

The fingers beneath her hand moved.

Sarine jumped, shock flooding her with nausea and warmth at the same time. "He moved!"

"Yes," the robot at his head said. "I am finishing the repairs on the consciousness unit."

Chills wrapped her arms. Her back knotted, spine rasping nerve clusters.

Sterling's eyes flashed on, then off. The second time, they stayed on, directed to Sarine. "Sarine, I had a dream," he said softly. "It was Green Forever and you were lost. You were calling my name."

Slowly, Sarine touched his lips with her fingers, soft almost warm, then clutched his smooth, cold hand tighter. Humans couldn't die and come back to life. But certainly robots could not dream.

"You're alive," she said, smiling.

*

Moltenrose

"You're late, boy," Rycoff mutters as I walk under the awning and into the tent. His belly hangs over an expensive gold belt, the vinyl trousers like a plastic sack he'd forced his flesh into. He wears a fashionable long-sleeved, bulky paper shirt. White. It sticks to his arms and back. There's already a little tear in it at the wrist. He goes through a dozen a day.

"How can I be? There's no line yet."

"I pay you by the hour, Ugly. Try to remember." He shuffles by me, leaving a scent-trail of sweat and mint. The black skin of his face glistens. The white braid that flaps over his shoulder is as artificial as my half-wig. A stranger might take him for a clown, but he's as shrewd a business-person as Colere the trans-hop queen, who owns half the Free World. Rycoff's just had a little less luck.

I take Main Street to work every day. It needs mending, as does the entire city of Moltenrose. Ghost City, people call it. A fitting place for me since I'm just one more broken down part of it. And the carnival on the east side where tourism keeps what's left of it alive is as good a place as any to work.

On the west side, the Tower where the Ignorant Army lives leans against the sky like a church. It's always dark. Sometimes I think no one really lives there but bats and sprites. But then my bio-pacer cuff, which regulates and protects my brainwave patterns, heats against my wrist and I know the unseen stimoceiver waves from our enemies in the Walled City are real, and that control of my own mind is due only to the slim bracelet sweating against my skin and the psi-gifted army in the Tower who fights to keep us free.

Every day I pass by the holosex bars, casinos, and street sellers vending everything from souvenirs to their own bodies. In the carnival itself, the tents are weather-stained, the rides blackened with oil and age. The Ferris wheel breaks down often, and all the seats are chipped. Rycoff says he can't afford to repaint. But he can afford the lights at night, the electricity to draw the assailable tourist eye.

He pays me shit. But it's work. **SEE THE HALF-MAN HALF-MONSTER,** the sign outside my tent reads. It's half-correct. For Rycoff, I wear a wig on the right side of my scalp, the side on which my face looks most normal. The left side, bulging and bumpy with tumors, is my monster side. I wear a clawed glove on my left hand. I'm supposed to take swipes at the gawkers, growling and grimacing all along. Most of the time, I just sit and stare at their stares. I don't mind. Finding pleasure is difficult enough without feeling guilty for it. If no one looked, I'd be out of a job.

The faces that come and go rarely interest me. I don't like looking at people with my entire attention. Their unmarred lips and perfect noses, smooth cheeks and shimmering hair irritate me. It's not their fault that I choose to look away from what I can never have. Just as they choose to look at what they never want.

After an hour, the air hotter than usual for these autumn months, I'm ready for a stim. Rycoff provides them as part of my wage. I try not to do more than four or five a day. They're expensive and I need money, not stims, to continue paying for my hemi-synch at home. And the rent.

I put out my **WILL RETURN IN TEN MINUTES** sign and go back inside. A cheap, bronze-gilt tapestry that comprises the background of my 'show' hides a table and a plastic lounge chair behind it. On the table lies a day's worth of cash. Beside it, four stim wafers have been set out in a line: purple, amber, cherry, black. Blacks are my favorite and I pocket it to save for last. I pass over the cherry and amber—they'll do nicely later—and palm the purple.

The wafer feels cool against my skin. With thumb and forefinger, I bring it to my lips, savoring sugar scent, faintly moist. Blood rushes in expectation. My fingers press the sides, lightly at first, teasing. Then with more strength. There is a popping sound as it breaks. Blue sparks. The sparks rush against my lips and into my mouth and I am swallowing light and energy and hope. All at once the scents and tastes are sweet and spice and leaf and dust. It all goes into me. I'm carried away on the silk air of bliss. That's where it's at. Inside. Everything that matters. The rest is all a play.

I come down fast, but the effects stay with me through my next set of people. I don't care about it being hot anymore. Or if the smooth faces moving in a line before me define a perfection I'll never have. They're looking at me now. Something's got them mesmerized. And I'm its center.

*

The illustrated girl outside the tattoo bar accosts me. Her bio-pacer, painted a rusty green, scratches my arm as she reaches out. "Hey, you could use a little color."

She's all colors. Brown, blue, green. Black-eyed. Somewhere in-between the ships and crosses, the robot warriors and damaged hearts, her true skin color appears jaundiced yellow. She wears only a bra and shorts. The tattoos obviously don't end where the clothing begins.

"No." I pull away. Yesterday, the accoster was a man. He started his sales pitch, loud and indifferent, until he really took a good look at me. In mid-sentence he stopped, then snarled, "Shit, you're already scarred enough." At least this girl treats me like everyone else.

"It'll be great," she says, raising her arms for emphasis. "Just do it. Maybe a flowing vine over your forehead. Or something feathery on your thigh…"

"I'm here for stims, that's all." But I smile at her. She's too young for all those pictures. Too little. I try to imagine the agony of all those need touches. If I think of my face, I can easily empathize.

But she shrugs, bored. "Oh. Mik has great stims today. A good price, too." She flips her long, dark hair forward and stalks off. She doesn't want my empathy. No one ever does. I'm too ugly.

I know Mik better than I'd like. Take a machine. Program it to defy and contradict every comment or question put to it. Give it no feeling, except perhaps bitter nonchalance. If Mik has searched for anything in life, it's reason to prove he has the one and only right to be miserable in the world. He laughs at stim-junkies, and at ugly-bugs like me because we're the shit of the earth and if it weren't for us, his life would be wonderful and he wouldn't be stuck in Moltenrose selling us stims. But obnoxious and vulgar as he is, we all still go to him for the best stuff this side of the Edge.

In the bar, against walls the color of burnt wood, dizzy holograms of Moltenrose in its prime—air shots, hill shots, skyline shots—I see Mik's hatchet-hacked mop of silver bobbing over a VR table. Through the smoke and low lighting, the show looks like lesbian porn. Tattoos cover the girls. It's only mildly interesting to me, since my fantasies favor men, but I approach and watch for a moment by his side, just to be polite. They're cute. It's not that I exclude women from my hemi-synch dreams; it's just that men have always interested me, perhaps from my standpoint of envying and coveting a more perfect male body. Being short, rather broad-shouldered and skinny-legged, not to mention the gruesome mountains of my face, I'll have to say my preferences have been limited to 'let's pretend'. So what I know of girls and boys is, of course, all limited to what my hemi-synch can give me. But the lesbians on Mik's table do not rouse my concupiscence.

After a moment, Mik freezes the show. "Ugly," he says without really looking at me, "you just get more hideous every day. Go away. Leave me alone. You just don't know what kind of day it's been."

"Sure," I say. "I can take my business somewhere else."

"You know," he says—his way of calling me back—"I think you should take all that money you make at carny and save it toward your face. Don't you think getting it fixed should be your priority? I mean, put yourself out of the rest of our misery. We all have to look at you, you know."

"Thanks for the advice." How many times has he said it? A hundred? Two hundred? It's all such a joke now. Still, there's a little part inside of me that pinches in pain. I ignore it. "And you're too perfect for all of us, so why aren't you taking your savings and getting out of this damned city?"

"I mean to, Ugly. Oh, I mean to. Maybe tomorrow. Maybe the next day. One day you'll come in here and I'll be gone. And you'll know I'm off having the time of my life."

"You aren't the kind of person who dreams."

He looks at me. "And you're what squirts out the wrong end of a dog. You can only dream, never touch." He laughs.

I shrug it off, needing to get down to business before I make myself sorry and try to punch him. "Got any blacks?"

"Saved 'em all for you, Ug." He pulls out a tube containing three blacks, five whites, and a purple. I can't afford all three blacks right now and he knows it. But I've got a black from Rycoff in my pocket. I can get two and save them for Tuesday when the carny's closed and I make nothing. Then I'll still have enough left over to buy the white for tomorrow morning until I get to work. And my spare black I can have tonight.

I give him almost all my money, take the stims and leave quickly, passing by a group performing their needle art on a prone man. Two are carving bloody hearts on his buttocks. I can feel the buzzing sound of their tools in my teeth. Not my pleasure.

The street outside looks long with dusk. It's still hot, but the sky overhead is dimmed blue, and to the west creased with orange. The air smells of the carnival: puke, spilled beer, woodsmoke and meat. If I concentrate, I can also smell taffy, popcorn and fried fish. My stomach grumbles in response. I've got insta-pacs at home. But that's not what I'm hungry for.

Even this far outside the Funzone the tourists make noise that carries on the air. There's music and screams, laughter and drums. The gambling establishments are the biggest draw. And the sex shows. But I've got the stims in my pocket. They're better than all this. I'm all too glad not to have to work evening tonight. Rycoff doesn't demand too much, so I can choose my hours. But it's getting plain I need another job. Rent is coming due. I can never make it on time, and each month I get further behind.

The street up to my place crumbles to gravel. The ground is littered with glass and broken stim wafers. It narrows to an incline, and rows of apartments and small houses, most burned and gutted, loom up several stories. Here it's quieter and weeds have broken through the underlying soil, ash-dusted. The sidewalks have become slabs of piled concrete, nearly impassable; but for all the ruin there is an occasional glimpse beyond fallen walls of a tangled rose garden gone wild, a dirt-buried fountain with a headless statue guardian, a wall mural of dolphins still standing though the structures all around it have collapsed. Anything of value has been long ago looted, and the Magistrate's guards manage to keep out gangs and wayward tourists. Still, it feel inhabited, haunted.

My place, a fixed up three-unit building, offers me a ground floor studio with a tiny side yard. The rent I can barely afford goes to the city's Magistrate who oversees the Tower and the psychic soldiers within. She does not even reside in the city and I can't help but resent the amount I have to pay to her each month. But I do have running water and a free dump card. And my neighbors are quiet.

As I pass by one of the more intact buildings, I hear a rustling sound—the wind perhaps, or rats—and stand still. A sharp bang makes me jump back, duck. Somewhere inside, a man yells something incomprehensible. There is a softer reply, more urgent, also male. The urgency rises to a scream.

I've heard screams all my life. The screams of lovers, of excited winners on the Midway, of anger. All are familiar to me. This is different, makes the skin along my spine freeze. I approach the blasted-out window of the building as quickly and quietly as I can. It's too shadowed to see anything, but the scream comes again, riveting. My toenails throb with it.

Climbing through the window proves to be noisy and awkward. My boot kicks a rusted pipe. I pick it up before it rattles more to give me away and hold it tightly in my left hand. Somewhere from the back, that same angry voice carries. The other voice is silent now. I move through a blackened hallway, my boot steps crunching loudly over soot and skeletal floorboards.

When I reach the back of the building I see a young man on the floor, hair spilling around his face like liquid copper. The face is smooth, gold as leaves, and I recognize him immediately as one of the more stunning body vendors who habituates the Midway's Main Street. I don't remember his name. Blood leaks from his nose and over one eye, and though his eyes are open, he's not moving…or breathing that I can see.

Standing over him is a man I don't recognize, soft-faced but with hard-eyes. He kicks the vendor in the side as I watch. The kid on the floor moans. Well, that's one breath at least.

I step forward, waving my pipe. "Hey!"

He looks up, light hair, sweat-drenched, streaking his face. "Get out of here!" he hisses. He wears a baggy, vinyl tank, tight vinyl trousers, black.

"You go!" I challenge.

"Or what, freak?" He comes at me.

Fighting is not my strength, but I find myself starting frays now and again on sheer spurts of adrenalin. Stupid *and* ugly.

"You want to die with him? Fine!"

"What'd he do to you?" I ask, trying to distract him.

"Changed his mind."

"I wonder why," I mutter.

"You—" And he comes at me, pulling out a scorebeam.

Against that weapon, I don't have a chance, but I leap on hope over a gaping hole in the floorboards. Hope that death'll be quick. Hope that the guy gets blood and soot all over himself. Hope that the pretty guy on the floor is already dead so he won't have to see me die without any grace at all.

But the beam's flame goes wild and, miraculously, my feet catch him at thigh-level and he goes down hard. I whack him as hard as I can with the pipe, and don't stop until it flies out of my slippery hands. I look down and see blood everywhere. My hands are red.

For a moment—only a moment—I don't understand. Then I step back as if moving outside myself, and survey the universe I've just created.

I've never killed a man before. The sensation is light, hot, nauseating. The taste of stale shock a bitter bouquet. My knees give way.

"Oh shit!" says a desperate voice to my left. "Fuuuuck!"

And damn, my mind adds, taunting. I don't know how to take this, but the brain kicks in with denial to help me out. "What? Hey?" Both legitimate questions. I glance at the pretty guy who's sitting up now, holding his bruised face in both hands. His hair washes over him like a tawny swab of light. I find myself thinking, for a second, of how I'd give anything to own that hair, how I've dreamed of having hair like that, or any hair at all. The man I have downed becomes an object of less concern.

"You killed him."

"I never...I didn't..." Not a great beginning by way of an introduction. Again the hair distracts me, all mirror, and antique gold with darker streaks of rust. It's chin-length in front, flowing long in back. He pushes it from his face, fingers rippling through it as if it were water.

"We gotta get out of here," he moans.

"Yeah. Yeah," I say, but make no move to stand.

He tries to get to his feet, falls once, then stands precariously. Blood drips onto his forehead and into his right eyebrow marring its perfect form. He grips his side and stumbles toward me. "We gotta go," he says again, the air coming out of him in thick breaths.

I'm remarkably light on my feet as I rise. My knees feel strong again. "Okay. My place is just up the street."

He comes up alongside me and I see the blood is flowing thicker on his forehead. "If I could just get cleaned up," he says.

"That cut needs attention."

"No," he interrupts, shaking his head.

"I don't have a holo-comm, but…"

"No!" He grabs my arms and pulls me toward the dark hall. "No holo-comm. That guy…you don't…" He inhales sharply, clutches his side again. "You don't know who he is!"

Was, my mind corrects. But I remain silent.

I don't remember making it up the broken street to my apartment, but I do remember a pink sky, a feeling of floating, a tight grip on my arm by a gasping man.

Once in my apartment, the first thing I see is how messy it is. "Sorry," I mutter, "'bout the mess. The sink's over there."

But he's already at the basin, my only washcloth pressed against a place just above his hairline. He's slim like a youngster, but tall. His clothing is light, shiny plastic, nearly see-through, and clings to him like a loose, second skin. The shirt is dark, forest green, a color that looks good on anyone, even me. But on him it hurts to see. He's far too pretty for a man.

With only one room, there's not much privacy. I sit on my unmade bed, the sheets yellow with wear and age. After a few minutes, and a few wring-outs of the cloth, he sits beside me, leaning into his hand where the blood still seeps into the cloth.

"Name's Kody," he says, very quietly.

"Zeth," I say, "but most people just call me Ugly."

At that, his lips curve up. A weak agreement, I think, until he asks, "Why?"

"Why? It's a goddamn nickname, that's all. The same way yours could be Beautiful."

The sun has fallen all the way now; I can tell by the tint of the windows: curried brown. Kody gets up slowly, moves toward one of them. He can't really be looking out, there's nothing to see but dead grass and a spindly knee-high tree I planted two years ago when I first moved in. His breathing's still high. I cross my arms and hunch into myself.

"Ugly's the man you just killed," he finally says. "You have the mind of a poet."

He's not looking at me; he's not moving a muscle, but the voice is loose and low. I laugh sharply. He's obviously delirious.

"People only see what's at the beginning of their vision," he continues. "That's the problem, don't you think?"

"Whatever you say, Beautiful," I reply. A hit on the head can make people babble. But the words snag me somewhere deep, like shadows and stims. Mind of a poet? Something quickens inside me, along with a lump of disappointment at my own gullibility.

"I don't expect you to understand," he replies.

"Well, you're raving."

"No. I'm a telepath. Undeveloped, of course, or I wouldn't be here selling things that ought not to be sold."

"Telepath?" I ask.

"I was turned down by the World Association for being only half-assed. They called me a half-path, but I can still sense thoughts. The man you killed was a Controller. I saw that in his thoughts. He was working for the Walled City. A spy. When he realized I was a 'path, he had to finish it. Now there'll be a hell of a lot of questions, thanks to you."

"Excuse me for saving your life."

He turns, a phantom of forest green, copper, bronze. "Thank you," he says. He puts his hand to the cut on his head. "And it's true. You have beautiful thoughts. I can't help it. They intrude."

My laugh is nervous this time. "Not fair. I can't read you."

"Better not to. Don't you know telepaths are wildly insane?"

"No."

He comes from the window and stands before me, hand still pressing the cut at his hairline. His bangs make a gold fringe against his wrist, red-tinged from the blood. His eyes hold antique light. "You have the most interesting face," he says.

Here it comes.

"No, really." He reaches out, touches the bumps with strong, firm fingers. I try not to flinch. I try not to be bitter, self-conscious, self-hating. Yet those feelings flip through me uncaught. He shakes his head. "No."

That one word shudders through me.

Then he says, "You're one of the most beautiful men I've ever met."

I can't help but turn to check my hemi-synch. The silver headband still hangs from a hook on the wall, untouched. And yet this all seems like a stim-dream of murder, seduction.

"Then telepaths must see things very differently from reality," I finally conclude.

"We do. Or maybe we see reality with more clarity than everyone else." His hand falls away. His voice is a breeze on thin, empty air.

I glance down suddenly. Between my legs: insistent, painful arousal. I can tell he's done it, somehow, with his thoughts, although completely unnecessary. I would never dispute my attraction to him.

"I don't have any money," I say quickly.

He kneels before me. His palm comes away from his head, fingers burnished with drying blood. It touches my now trembling knee. "Did I ask for money?"

Later, his golden hands form a secret language of messages on my body. One of the messages reads: "Thank you for saving my life." Another reads, impossibly: "You are beautiful."

*

Beautiful won't go out the next day. "Too many people saw me go with the Controller," he says. "I have to wait until it all blows over."

"Well, I still have to go to work." I can't ignore the fact that the rent is due and I've spent most of it on stims. And though he made me forget all my troubles last night, now I can't stop thinking of the killing and all the blood. The excuse of self-defense doesn't temper the memory.

"I have money," he says, reading my mind. "I'll pay your rent, whatever you want. Just please let me stay." He stands by the window again, looking at my sick little yard. His hands are clutched behind his back. He's naked to the waist. A tremble moves over the hard muscles of his back. My breath catches.

"I have no intention of throwing you to the wolves," I reply.

When he turns, he's smiling. "I knew you wouldn't."

I leave, still trying to figure out if he made himself tremble on purpose, if my mind is still really my own. That's some weapon he has, body and mind combined. I try not to forget that even as I'm still reeling fresh from murder, fresh from losing my virginity.

*

Nothing appears changed on the outside, and yet everything is. I've killed. I've taken my first lover.

The carnival is brighter, less dark. All the tourists look fresh and alive. When they stare at me, I'm different, too, and I even fancy I see some of them leaving the tent with their faces creased in disappointment.

When I think of Kody, my body heats. I forget all about having killed a man. I don't have the craving for as many stims. With the ones left over from yesterday, and the ones Rycoff gives me today, I figure I'm stockpiling. I take my cash and instead of heading to the tattoo bar at the end of my shift, I buy a bag of bread, some cheese. There's money left, and for once I'm not worried about the rent. I buy a silver band for my thumb, a piece of jewelry I've been wanting for months. When I put it on, I feel less like myself, more like a man who's just emerged from a cocoon.

As I walk home, I turn onto my street and stop fast, my packages suddenly slippery in my now sweating hands. Just up the jumbled road, the ruin where we left the Controller's body is surrounded by people in expensive clothes. Two flyers are parked in the middle of the street, a strange sight since only government employees and officers of the World Association are allowed to own them. Panic turns my throat sour. I can't go home now. They'll follow. They'll question. And they'll find Beautiful, imprison me. I turn around and head straight back to the carnival.

"I can't afford to keep you on extra hours tonight," Rycoff says gruffly. It's a lie, of course. He's very wealthy. "What's the matter with you? Go home."

I stand there with my hands still full of the food I bought. The tent is dark, closed. "I'll open for a few hours for free," I offer.

Rycoff frowns, reddish-black creases forming between his eyes as he stares down at me. "You're loony, but do what you like. I'm not paying for it. And mind you don't tip yourself out of the ticket sales, either."

"I wouldn't dream of it," I mutter, quickly entering the shadowed interior—sweet smell of dust, damp mold. It's hot inside, and I fling open the front of the tent to air it out, then light the fuses in the gas lamps. Rycoff could afford electricity here, but he thinks the eerie lanterns are a better atmosphere for monsters. Their luminescence flickers against the sloped walls and ochre dirt floor like a gently rolling, orange sea. Big velvet moths appear seemingly from nowhere, called from their shadows to find their end in the lamp flames. Would that I had such purpose.

Rycoff sends a ticket-tearer to my door—a girl I haven't seen before with strange, scared eyes—and as I put the sign out, she stares at me, her long, adolescent fingers gripping and crinkling her white paper skirt. "It's not that bad a job," I say to her. She looks quickly away, shrugging.

I go into the tent, don my wig and glove, and sit. I'm open for business.

Worry makes the time go slow. I wonder if Kody is still in my studio. And I keep thinking maybe I left behind evidence in the building where the Controller died.

About an hour into it, with only about twenty customers so far, the girl starts lingering inside the doorway. She's still afraid, but her hands have stopped worrying her clothes. Her mirror-sandals pick up the lamplight, making her feet look as if they are on fire. Finally, she speaks.

"Why do you do it?"

"I get just as hungry as you," I reply.

She has tightly curled black hair. It sponges at her bare shoulders. The sleeveless white paper pullover she wears is too big. One strap keeps falling down her brown arm.

"But you're not getting paid tonight. I heard Rycoff…"

"And that's none of your business," I interrupt.

She kicks the dirt floor. It floats up, settling in a faint, yellow sheen on her sandals. The sounds of the Midway ghost in like psychic broadcasts. Moths click against the glass of the lanterns; some find their true paths and suicide in the blanched heat, sizzling into oblivion.

She gets up the nerve to ask more questions, but my mind wanders. My throat tightens every time I imagine Kody getting caught by those officers with the aircar, his long body folded and broken by ankle-wrist chains, his hair getting caught in the door as they slam it and carry him away to a distant fate.

But they can't know he's one of two involved in murder. How would they? Kody's too smart. He wouldn't have left a trail, not for any of his customers. He wouldn't have told anyone where he was going. Would he?

It's all too crazy. I have to go home now and find out. I get up from my chair. The girl—I still don't know her name—is telling me something about her twin sister who's handicapped, and how she could never imagine her sibling parading her deformation for money. "It would just be, well, *awful!*"

"Honey," I say, grabbing my sacks of food from the back, turning out the lamps, "awful is where we live. You don't have to imagine it. It's here, all around us. Your sister knows, why don't you?" I move past her. She's blinking hard, pushing the falling strap up her arm for the hundredth time.

"It's okay," she says nervously. "I'll close up. You look like you're in a hurry."

I can see tears in her eyes. And I'm thinking, *Where the fuck planet did she come from?* All the while my heart is hammering out in code: KODY.

My street is empty, the blackened apartment buildings yawning, shadow-bits clinging to their broken-window teeth. No sign of the aircars. Or the expensive-clad government people. No sign of any life at all, save insectoid and rodent. As I pass the dolphin mural, the only eyes that watch me are from those sea-mammals, friendly, black, lifted somehow outside time. Not flames or weather or vandals have marred their beauty. Yet.

But everything beautiful goes away. I tell myself this as I pass by the very building where my first murder, only a day old, now haunts the ripped walls. I tell myself this as my boots crunch gravel and broken stims, as I approach my dark hovel I know will be empty.

No lights. No sound. Why would I think it would be any different? It's better to have no hope in a world such as this, so as not to wear the big, scared eyes of teenage ticket-tearers who think they understand what it means to breathe and walk in the dust of Moltenrose where at any time a psychotronic war could break out full force and our minds be squeezed from their fragile shells.

I tell myself that unhappiness is a right you can't escape. I'm always wanting what I can't have. That's my final flaw, far deeper than any mottling that may drench my face.

The gloom runs out around my arms and feet like smoke when I unlock the studio door. Silence. But for the slow drop of my rusted faucet. Termites nesting in the walls.

My bags slip from my sweating hands. I clench my forefinger to my thumb, feel it slip against cool metal, the just-bought ring like a seam of tender, new soul I'd almost let escape.

I'd tell all butterflies, if I could, to never stretch their wings. They'll only die.

The air in my lungs scrapes up my throat, out. So, this is where I have lived. The former me. The new me. How ugly. Ugly.

My hemi-synch hangs, glinting on the wall. Kody could still be alive in there, in binaural, synthesized reverie, but that thought only gives me bitter succor. The room is too small. My boots tear at a decaying rug set, like an afterthought, against stained floorboards. A single, ancient, cushioned armchair is all that greets me, little squat creature rescued from a collapsed cottage. It had lived a lonely life for awhile, overlooking the dirt-buried fountain down the street, until I found it. Until I lugged it home.

When I breathe in, it is as if my lungs can no longer hold the air they are meant to take in. The perspiration of my life has sunk deeply into the walls, the floor, the ceiling, until all I can smell is myself, the salted sighs, lost sugar-dreams.

My eyes blink back pain even as my mouth spreads into the familiar rictus-grin I always greet the dark with.

Then the bed moves. I imagine it. I am dreaming awake.

But, "Hey," the mattress says. "Why're you just standing there making faces? And where've you been?"

I nearly drop to the floor in surprise. Catching myself, I blurt, "I thought..."

"I know," he replies. "Think too much." He holds out his arms.

His skin is like cool silk. He wriggles naked against me everywhere he can reach. His lips melt against the lumps on my face. I think of painted dark sea-eyes. Maybe there are still places in this world where beauty can be caught, can be saved. Where nothing can mar it, not the elements, not lonely years and ashen suns, not dark.

"Of course there are," Kody reproaches, telepathically stroking the hidden blooms of my mind.

*

Author's Note

The novella and short story comprising these pages are set in the universe of my novel *Pale Zenith*.

While the novel, novella and story all stand alone, if one were to put them in chronological order it would look like this:

Moltenrose
Green Forever
Pale Zenith

Technically, this book is a prequel to the novel. But the stories need not be read in any order. I placed *"Moltenrose"* last in this collection simply because the mood of the ending was the mood I wanted to leave the reader with.

I hope if readers of this book have not read *Pale Zenith*, they may be inspired to look it up. It is a novel of tenderness, tragedy, abduction, betrayal, coming of age, loss, love and…spychiatrists! By design, I am rich on the characterization side in the art of writing in the hopes that readers will come to care about the people in my books as much as I do.

Thank you for reading.

If you have time, please think about reviewing this book on Amazon.

For more information about my other books and collections, visit my Amazon author page. Visit my blog at: http://wendyrathbone.blogspot.com/

Wendy Rathbone

Addendum

Special Bonus: Two Poems

A note from the author: *I often compose poetry to inspire my stories and novels, before, during and after writing the books. Here are two from my* **Pale Zenith** *universe.*

An 'Ugly' Poem

*(set in the **Pale Zenith** universe)*

On the fiery wind,
a secret wind
of grief
and dead seas,
I hear the lost ones call
to each other
as they scavenge
each other's dreams.

In a city of ruined autumns
I live
upon the broken Earth
above the ordinary cries
of Edge ghosts
clutching sorrow, evanescent,
clutching air
dry as rust.

The city sleeps.
Its dreams pull forward
on the leash of the moon.
Stars fall

like ships in the night.

My lover,
mirror of my opposite self,
companion, partner, brother
leaves roses in my mind
with telepathic thoughts.

I ask the Magistrate
who lives in a holographic
projection
if I can guard the streets,
protect what's left
of Moltenrose.
She laughs. I am
too small.
Too ugly.

In a dingy basement
I see an android destroy
a spychiatrist.
I bring the Magistrate
the leftover pieces.

Now I guard the streets
but no one cares.
I haunt the falling buildings,
whisper secrets,
show mercy to strangers. Here
in the ancient skeletons of
an old city crumbled by the
technologies of war
everyone's forgotten wonder,
the dream of the future
as distant
as waking love.

After The Seven-Day War

*(set in the **Pale Zenith** universe)*

The wind scrapes across
dead towers,
flowing into the lamplight
of your hair.
An elder sun of
melted rubies
turns glass to blood.
Lightning etches
secret codes
upon the ash of sky.
At night the moon
walks the old ravines
searching
for little husks of stars.

Preview of the novel: *Pale Zenith*

Pale Zenith

by

Wendy Rathbone

Prologue
The World Outside the Walled City (Parallel Earth)

The park looked lush and full in the late evening. All the trees seemed thicker at night, heavier. The plush lawns soaked up dense shadows, black and green mixing to form shades of sage and raw pewter. The air smelled of pine-resin and flame.

On the horizon, beyond the wall of trees, there had been a fire earlier in the day. Lightning had started it, some reports said. Others speculated someone had deliberately set it. Someone from The Walled City, a psychic soldier, had projected the flames onto the vulnerable farm land outside Tiem, one of the biggest cities of the Free World. But the flames were out, now. And all psychotronic defense systems were on standby alert. The World's own psychic soldiers were no doubt actively probing the night skies overhead, looking to meet and battle any more errant attacks.

"*If* it was an attack," Tira said to her two friends, leaning against the back of a dew- damp, wooden bench, "it wasn't aimed very well. There had been reports of thunderstorms in the area, so everyone could be jumping to conclusions." She'd studied psychotronics in college for the past two years and found the science to be inexact at best, and not a little mystifying.

"Still, we shouldn't be out tonight of all nights." Jorik would not sit, his nervousness showcased by the way his fists bunched in the deep pockets of his vinyl trousers. His pale bangs scattered across his forehead like shimmering mothwings. He, too, was a student scientist. Where Tira was driven by curiosity, Jorik empowered himself with fear. The emotion made him appear smaller than his tall stature.

"Why don't you go back, then, Jorik? We'll catch up to you later," said Cassus.

Tira turned to the third person in their party. Cassus was watching her with bold, dark eyes. He'd never made it a secret that he wanted her, never held back from assessing her to her face, never seemed to understand fully that her rejection of him was rejection. She had eyes only for Jorik, and Cassus knew it, but still he followed them around, pretending friendship for the other man that was clearly a fabricated excuse to be closer to her, pretending to show an interest in the new group marriages that were 'all the fashion, now', perhaps to intimidate her into giving in to him, or to undermine Jorik's already thin ego.

"I don't want to go back alone," Jorik replied, kicking at the ground. "Come on you two. Curfew was set for a reason."

"We're safest tonight," Tira said softly to him. "You know that. When the armies are on alert, the chance of anything breaking through their barriers is far less. We're fine here. And we're under the cover of these trees." She felt a soft wind blow as she said that, scented with distant ash. Her spine suddenly tingled.

"You've read the reports," Cassus added. "We all have in Strategy 101. The easiest victims are those who lose their bio-pacers. And those who are purposely targeted for political reasons. We're just students." He fingered the silver cuff at his wrist.

"Fools," Jorik said. "Yeah, I read those reports. People are attacked at random, too. And some deaths that have been reported as accidental might not be that at all. You saw the one where the little girl was hit on the head by a potted plant that fell, for no known reason, from a high shelf. And Supreme Justice Kiki died of unknown causes in her own bed. She was 44! Bio-pacers didn't save them."

"They can't prove it was an attack," Tira said, looking at

her own bio-pacer, a strip of silver on her left wrist that helped block the constant bombardment of mind-control waves coming from the enemy. "But those are isolated and rare cases. You know that."

"That's how war is." Cassus' teeth showed. Tira wondered how he could smile so often and so much. It was as if he took nothing seriously.

"The Walled City's Ignorant Armies track better at night," Jorik said. "We should go home. Everyone's safer indoors. They've always taught us that."

"Supreme Justice Kiki wasn't safe in her own bed. Besides, I hate locking myself away every night. Isn't the park beautiful?" Tira asked.

Jorik turned away.

Cassus kept grinning at her. "Lovely. I'd take you here every night if you were mine."

Jorik turned abruptly as several shadows scattered across the huge lawns. "Hey – "

Tira saw instantly they were only a group of children running into the trees. "Stupid," she muttered. "When I was small I belonged to a night-gang once. It was a way of defying the truth, the war. We practically held seances to invite the enemies to psychically attack us. Nothing ever happened. We were harmless, so we were ignored."

"No one is harmless in a war. We're all soldiers in a way," Jorik said. "And aren't we doing, right now, exactly what you say those children are doing? Defying the odds, challenging."

"Yes." Tira reached out to touch Jorik's arm. "And sometimes soldiers take risks. Sometimes they just have to feel the night air on their skin, have a little fun, a little wildness."

"Sit down with us, Jorik. I'm your friend. I won't let anything happen to you," Cassus said, the sweetness in his voice making Tira wince.

The tall, pale man looked unsure. That trait of indecision was his least endearing characteristic. Finally, he sat on the other side of Cassus much to Tira's consternation, head bowed. How had Cassus won him over so easily? Was Jorik so blind? She shook her head, deciding it was time to find new friends.

The breeze picked up. "Doesn't that feel good?" she asked.

"Hmmm," Cassus said.

Jorik merely stated, "I have physics homework I should be doing."

Tira leaned back, letting her long hair flow behind the back of the bench. The dampness of the evening clung to the wood and cooled the back of her neck. She still smelled distant flames, and wondered how the scent could seem to be growing stronger with every breath. But she ignored her thoughts, the night lulling her, too lovely to ruin with anymore questions.

The Walled City (Parallel Earth)

In the War Room on the top floor of The Walled City's ruling palace, the pretty park with its three unusual inhabitants took over the main imaging monitor.

"Make the pictures clearer!" the head controller, Stannos, ordered. "I want to hear every word." He watched as his number one controller ordered the spychiatrist machine who manipulated his 'seer' girl's talents to refine the image. The girl was young tonight, barely twelve. Her name was Lacy. Stannos' spychiatrists had found her on an alternate Earth in an alternate timestream, and identified her special abilities immediately, as they had been programmed to do. He used her often at varying ages, his spychiatrists able to traverse time as easily as space and dimension, stealing her from the other realm, the other Earth, mostly at night as she slept. Her family never missed her. She was one of his best 'seer' spies. And, in fact, at an older age, the girl had been personally interesting to him as well. Having his spychiatrists program her for sex was as simple as using her for war. And it gave Stannos a heady, powerful feeling to do just that.

The girl cried out as the spychiatrist prodded her obscenely between the legs with one of its clawed appendages. Pain made her ability stronger. The picture on the monitor became a close-up, the conversation loud and clear.

"Good," Stannos said. "Good." He watched as the students conversed. He laughed when he learned they were students of psychotronics. That admission alone had just garnered them a death sentence.

Stannos turned to another Controller further across the room. "Do you have Mr. Smith ready?" he asked.

"He's in perfect agony. The spychiatrist is holding him back, but as soon as it has your coordinates and lets him go, he'll project powerfully."

"Then he's working strong tonight?"

"He's in top shape. Any preferences on mode of execution?"

"Hmmm." Stannos fingered his long, black braid. A royal blue ribbon wove through it, glistening silk. "You know how I abhor complexities. A quick death will be best for them. Let's try Mr. Smith's talent for long-distance telekinesis. Can he drop that nearby tree on them, do you think? Their bio-pacers can't defend them against a falling tree."

The Controller studied the monitor. "With the ease and grace of a natural disaster," he replied.

"Good. I've got the distractions in place. Their skies are busy tonight with prowlers. They've got their soldiers on alert." He looked at his half-dozen distractors, all controlled by yet another spychiatrist, waiting to do telepathic battle. It would be rough on them. He expected to have at least one or two casualties, but these were the expendable ignorants, the ones he didn't have to count on as more than mere pawns. The youngest was a boy of about eight. The older ones, three women, two men, had less refined talents, but would fool the prowlers long enough for Mr. Smith to fell his tree, and long enough for Lacy to keep 'seeing' until he could be sure the job was done.

"All right," he said. "Let's do it." He ordered his spychiatrist to begin prodding his six until their minds soared beyond the walls of the city. They moaned and cried out as their psyches projected into an ethereal battle. The pain made them aggressive and strong, not weak, though their anguish filled the War Room with stunning screams. My army, Stannos thought, grinning. Who'd have thought it? Children and weaklings alike, made to be strong as the most honed of fighters.

On the main monitor, over the park, a squiggle of green lightning lit up the sky.

"Now!" he yelled.

The students on the monitor jumped up from their bench, crying out in surprise. But it was too late for them. Mr. Smith's unblocked lightning had gotten through and struck the exact tree Stannos had wanted targeted.

"Precision," he called out. "That's what I like to see!"

The tree fell toward the small group, catching two of them straight on the heads. Their skulls popped like balloons, crushing. The third one of their party, Jorik the cowardly one, miraculously avoided being hit. Stannos watched him run screaming through the long shadows and the plush night-silvered grass.

"Follow him?" the Controller asked.

Lacy's mind seemed to be losing him. Jorik grew more distant on the monitor, though his yells flew up into the air and through the speakers of the War Room to mix with Stannos' distractors.

"Yes."

Lacy's spychiatrist prodded her with a claw again, and bathed her in blue light. Her drugged screams heightened, shrill and young. The runner on the monitor grew more distinct, until her vision seemed to follow directly at his heels.

One of Stannos' six, a woman with plump hips wearing a flannel nightgown, fell dead to the floor. Blood poured from her nose and ears.

"Hurry!" Stannos cried out. "He's getting away!"

Lightning flashed at Jorik, hitting him in the back. He flew forward, airborne for about eight feet, then fell. His bio-pacer glowed, absorbing some of the energy, and miraculously he got up, shaken, but still alive.

"Damn it! Have Mr. Smith try again!"

Just then Lacy gasped, cried out, "No!" and fainted. The monitor went blank.

"We've lost him," the Controller said.

Stannos' fingernails, long and pointed, cut into his palms as he tried to control his rage. Another of his distractors fell. He couldn't tell if the man was dead or unconscious.

"That's it then," he finally said, ordering his spychiatrist to let the others go. "We need more people if we want to do more damage. But for tonight we got the job done. Jorik will tell everyone what he saw. They'll know it wasn't an accident. They'll fear us even more, as they should. And when I amass my gifted soldiers all at once, nothing will be able to stand against them. The whole World both inside and outside The Walled City will be ours."

Part I - Earth (Present Day)

Chapter One

Lacy met Zack and Leo in the city. Country-bred herself, their eyeliner decorated eyes and slow smiles surprised her at first. The fact that they were identical twins made them seem even stranger.

"I have no scruples," Zack said, a dubious introduction.

"I can vouch for that," Leo added.

She could only nod in mute fascination as they bought her several rum and Cokes in a row. Something hollow widened inside her. A neglected child within. A void made of time and stillness that kept her separate from humanity, made her always think of herself as a fringe element on the outside looking in.

Their shoulder-length hair was so brown it was almost green. Every time one of them turned away from her, the light would hit it, illuminating more autumn colors: wheat, applerose, mulch. She'd never seen hair that moved as if alive.

"I know what it is like to be killed," Leo said.

"I can vouch for that." Zack snickered, his languid brown eyes rolling like marbles in triangular sockets. He was drunk. He fingered his phone, glancing at it now and again.

Lacy rarely patronized bars. She hated that scene. What drew her to *Sergio's* this night, after a long day at *Burger Buster,* was still a mystery. But these two...they were *terrible.* Not hard, not mean-looking, just terrible in the way they finished each other's sentences, the way they laughed at their own jokes. There were two of them, yet they somehow seemed as one. They were a solution to some bizarre, indefinable urge she'd always denied, and she fell easily, delicately in love with them.

At the time, though, she never would have named her response 'love.' She had no answers in her life, no easy definitions for behavior and emotion. Everything seemed to function, breathe, dance, surge around her, but never with her. She'd fallen away from ritual and meaning a long, long time ago.

It seemed these two had fallen out of the pattern, too.

"How do you know what it's like to be killed?" she asked.

"He had a nightmare once," Zack answered for his brother. The way she could tell them apart at first was that Zack had his black blazer sleeves rolled up. Leo's sleeves covered all but the tips of his fingers. The cuffs dangled on the bar top absorbing condensation. The fact that Zack was the more forward – the controller – of the two, also was not lost on her.

"The hell it was." Leo leaned into his kelp-hued drink. "No nightmare I ever had left marks."

Lacy's stomach went cold. The rum and Cokes she'd drank started to awaken inside her. "What kind of marks?"

"Let's just say Zack and I aren't quite identical anymore." Leo didn't look up. His drink held his world. He stared at it for a long time.

Her shoulders hunched, and a chill etched along her spine like a fleshless finger probing, penetrating through her careful human-normal veil. "What kind of marks?" she asked again.

"He's drunk. He don't like to talk about it," Zack said when Leo didn't answer. "Don't know why he brought it up now. He never talks like this."

Her glance at Zack was more desperate than she'd intended to show. For a moment, she wished him away. "Please." As the separate core of herself continued to expand, Lacy's mind started flashing back. The country. Her grandparent's farm. Feeling unsafe. Sure she was being watched all the time.

Her skin squirmed in that same way now. Was it happening again? She held onto the counter edge, the polished wood slipping against her palms, and glanced nervously over her shoulder. Everything felt wrong, as it had many times back on the farm just before something strange would happen: a nightmare, a whispering voice, a peripheral glimpse of a ghost. Was it only the drinks?

"He's got scars and things, that's all," Zack said matter-of-factly, still speaking for his brother.

"Scars?" she prompted, ignoring Zack by leaning around him on the bar, by trying to get Leo to look up.

"From nothing I did," Leo murmured, brown eyes flashing up, then down again toward his drink.

"They happened while he slept," Zack added. "His dreams sometimes leave real marks. Right?" He leaned off-balance toward Leo, who nodded without looking up. Lacy's view was cut off by his shoulder.

"You mean you dream something hurts you, like a punch in the face, and then wake up with a bloody nose?" Her skin was prickled, rough. She thought of getting up, going to the other side of Leo so Zack couldn't interfere. But before she could move, she felt shock coat the back of her throat in dry layers as Leo answered.

"No." Leo turned and leaned on his upturned palm, staring past Zack, who had pulled back slightly, and right into Lacy's eyes. "No, not like that at all."

"Just scars," Zack said, touching the counter, his rings clinking against it. "You know, already healed."

Her breath came out slow and cool-scented from the alcohol.

So, she wasn't alone. Someone else had experienced what she had. Someone else had nightmares that left real wounds in their wake. Wounds that had no outside explanation. But it was all too coincidental. Perhaps Leo had drawn her here. Or someone had. The sense of wrongness had not faded. Someone was watching. She knew it. Felt it. Leo had gone back to watching his drink. Zack's fingers still pestered the bar top with abstract designs.

The bar looked normal. Kids played pool on the upper deck, cigarettes dangling from mouths and fingers like captured fireflies. Others chatted on the cell phones or squinted at laptops in the dimness. Smoke choked the air. Lovers occupied booths. A couple of young girls were slow-dancing by the jukebox, one with a shaved head and long, mylar earrings, the other with a ponytail dyed crow-black.

But Lacy wasn't entirely reassured. Any one of them could be someone or some *thing* other than what they appeared. Her paranoia itched again. She could almost 'see' beyond the fabric of air that something, some presence just hovered there, eavesdropping. That feeling...she thought she'd escaped it by leaving the farm. But now...

"Hey," Zack was saying. "Hey." He snapped long, sharp-nailed fingers in front of her eyes. The pinky nail was painted black. He wore two silver bands, one on his little finger, one on his ring finger. Leo's hands were covered by his jacket, so she couldn't see if he wore the bands, too.

"Sorry." She blinked and looked down. "What kind of marks?" she asked again. The conversation had gotten too personal too fast, but she couldn't stop. Alcohol deadened her careful inhibitions.

"Why so insistent?" Zack asked.

She wanted Leo to talk to her, not the protective, sardonic brother's keeper.

As if reading her thoughts, Leo looked up. His unguarded gaze settled on her. Not appraisal. More, curiosity. And, perhaps, fear. "Yeah," he finally said. "Why so insistent?" When he asked the question, it held a less accusatory tone.

"I had nightmares that left scars, too."

"Shit," Zack said.

Leo simply stared at her.

After that, they surrounded her for the rest of the evening, twin slim shadows like wings that stayed unfurled. Two guardian angels to her right and to her left.

She felt warmer being with them. An instant kinship linked them, a familiarity that was especially strong between herself and Leo.

Safety in numbers, she thought, clasping both their hands as they headed for the door at closing.

Outside it was a clear, summer evening. While they walked, she thought of the past.

~

Fragmentary whirlwinds. Nausea. The scent of needles.

The little girl, Lacy, closed her eyes. "What world is this?" she asked.

No response.

Footsteps. She saw no one. But a voice in her mind, a soft wind murmuring, said: Close your eyes.

Something hurt her between her legs. She screamed.

Then she was reading a book, but her eyes were still closed. She scanned the cover. *Webs New Ion.* The rest faded. She opened the book to the middle. The words blurred on the page. Then cleared. *Lapel, part of a garment folded back, lapidary, a cutter of gemstones, lapis lazuli, azure, opaque,*

88

semi-precious, lapse, to fall away, lapwing, crested plover, larceny, theft, larch, cone-bearing tree, lard, the melted and clarified fat, larder, large, lariat, lark, larvae, larynx, lascivious, laser, lash... A break. Then a line jumped out: *Ha-ha from hell...*

None of it made sense until the last sentence, which startled her. Her eyes flew open. Hurting bright light. Metal hands. Chapped touches and footsteps. Scent of burnt oil.

She woke crying and shivering in her own bed. When she'd first had this dream at age eight, she'd known it wasn't right, wasn't normal. Now she was eleven and the dream still came. In the notebook she kept by the bed, she wrote what she could remember from the book.

Ha-ha from Hell.

The dream took her mind, squeezed it. She wrote to reclaim what was lost. She wrote to understand as the middle flesh between her legs began again to ache. Something had touched her there, not a hand or a person, but a tool.

But when she got up to go to the bathroom there was only a little blood. Nothing to wake anyone for. Nothing to worry Grandmother about. After all, some girls her age had already started to menstruate. Perhaps that was all it was, though intuitively she knew better.

When she looked out her bedroom window into the deep night of farm country, nothing moved. Not even the moon which seemed to be hanging like a hook suspended on a chain very close – too close – to her rectangle window.

She imagined a big man floating in the sky, holding onto a pole with his night-line cast down onto the flowing, liquid land. The hook would snag whatever was in its path.

She jumped out of sight of it and dived under cotton sheets, homemade quilts and fluffy animals. In the center of the bed she curled into herself, making herself so small that nothing in the night could find her.

(Look for this novel in trade paper or ebook on Amazon.com.)

ABOUT THE AUTHOR

 Wendy Rathbone has had dozens of stories published in anthologies such as: Hot Blood, Writers of the Future (second place,) Bending the Landscape, Mutation Nation, A Darke Phantastique, and more. Over 500 of her poems have been published in various anthologies and magazines. She won first place in the Anamnesis Press poetry chapbook contest with her book "Scrying the River Styx." Her poems have been nominated for the Science Fiction Poetry Association's Rhysling award at least a dozen times.

Her recent books include:

"Pale Zenith," science fiction novel

"The Foundling," male/male romance novel

"None Can Hold the Dark," sequel to "The Foundling"

"The Secret Sharer," science fiction romance novella

"Unearthly," omnibus collection of 7 out-of-print poetry booklets

"The Vampire Diaries: The Myth," available from Kindle Worlds

"The Vampire Dairies: Deep In the Virginia Woods," available from Kindle Worlds

"My House Is Full of Whispers," erotica short story collection

"Letters To An Android," science fiction novel

"Turn Left at November" poetry collection

"Beneath the Blue Dusk and the Sea" fantasy and science fiction short story collection

She lives in Yucca Valley, CA with her partner of 34 years, Della Van Hise.

LETTERS TO AN ANDROID
Wendy Rathbone

Cobalt is a created human, vat grown and born adult, with no human rights and indentured to serve others for the duration of his life. Liyan is a young man with wanderlust in his eyes, embarking on a career that takes him to the furthest regions of space. The two become unlikely friends and create a memorable long-distance correspondence. Through Liyan, Cobalt gets to explore the universe, living vicariously through his friend's wave transmissions. A strong bond develops between them that not even the stars can put asunder.

Now you know an android who writes poetry.

This is all your fault. Did you not read my last wave telling you extracurricular activities for my kind are discouraged? Of course this is harmless and strangely enjoyable and does not necessarily require me to leave the hotel. Pel would not care if I wrote lines of equations or nonsensical juxtaposed words. As long as the act does not bring my mental state into question.

However, in history, poetry is often written by the rebels.

So we can keep this to ourselves.

Let me know about your lieutenant's test.

And to give you peace of mind, I never believed you observed me as anything other than human.

Some people are and always will be hateful bigots. Most people are simply uncomfortable in speaking to "property." And anyway, friendship, like poetry, is also discouraged.

Your friend,

Cobalt

From the author: www.eyescry.com/html/publications.htm
On Amazon:
http://www.amazon.com/Letters-Android-Wendy-Rathbone-ebook/dp/B00LNE7BMM/

PALE ZENITH
Wendy Rathbone
A Science Fiction Novel

On a far-flung "Earth" in a parallel universe, two factions are fighting a decades-long psychic war. Young talented psychics are being temporarily kidnapped from present day Earth, seemingly at random, to serve as part of one side's psychic army. They are put under the control of spychiatrists, mysterious machines with many limbs that have a programmed ability to travel time and space and universes to kidnap and control carefully selected humans. The humans never know they are being used; when their missions are completed they are brought back to their universe through time and placed back in their beds, their memories wiped.

————————

The shadows wound the tall corridor in muted gold, varnished brown. It seemed as though they were in the bowels of a giant serpent coiled outside time, outside space.

When they left the palace, a familiar sun flourished in a clear, blue sky. But this wasn't their sun. Not Zack's sun. It was an alien star burning within a different galaxy in an all too distant universe. Zack looked up squinting, trying to see if he could peer beyond the sky, beyond the pale of midday and into his own timespace, but there was nothing. Only sunlight. Only the thin atmosphere of an Earth not his own.

His back knotted again. Leo's presence was a gelid space inside his chest, empty. Always before he'd felt a warmth there, a sort of pressure like someone's hand pressed gently to his heart. He'd taken Leo for granted knowing, the way a shadow falls when you block the sun, that he was there around him, inside him: blood, air, salt, brain, soul. They were genetic duplicates, twins, spiritual halves. Without him, Zack knew the first icy tugs of panic.

From the Author:
http://www.eyescry.com/html/publications.htm

On Amazon:
http://www.amazon.com/Pale-Zenith-Wendy-Rathbone-ebook/dp/B00DRHMB00/

The Foundling
by Wendy Rathbone

Diego is a powerful man with a tragic past. Out on the expansive ocean in his private yacht, he discovers a beautiful and mysterious man adrift on a raft, near death. The bond that forms between them in the aftermath of Alec's rescue is one of fierce passion, though lacking in trust. Can they make it work, or will Alec's amnesia bring forth secrets so disturbing as to tear them apart? A passionately erotic love story of desire and darkness, exquisite and explicit.

I can see his struggle between gratitude and uneasiness. He is buffeted by all things new and strange. He does not know where he is from, who he is or what happened to him. He does not know me. There has not been enough time to transition between strangers and friendship.

This isolation of his is something I can identify with, but it is also a feeling no one can help him with until or unless he gets his own life back. And his memory.

If that doesn't happen, then it will take time for him to build a new life. He is polite to me, even friendly, but even a night together during a storm with his arms wrapped tight around my waist doesn't calm the surge I see inside him, the emptiness, the loss, possibly even panic. That night may have reinforced some trust in me, but so far not enough for him to completely relax.

He seeks me out, though. That's something. He sits by me at dinner when he can have any seat of his choosing. I watch him closely when he does not realize it. At dinner the following night after we had only 'slept' together, and before we go to bed again in separate rooms, I notice everything about him, how he moves, the way the air warms when he is closer to me, the dry sheen of his lips as they part for more air when he is reacting to something, or speaking, or eating.

His hands still shake. Anyone else might not notice because he keeps them clasped into fists at his sides or, while sitting, pressed tight to his lap.

I spend another fretful night alone. I dream restlessly, wild, loud and colorful visions I cannot recall at all as soon as my eyes open. All I know is the dreams leave me unfulfilled, impatient.

FROM THE AUTHOR:

www.eyescry.com/html/publications.htm

On Amazon:

http://www.amazon.com/Foundling-Wendy-Rathbone-ebook/dp/B008E97SOA/

None Can Hold the Dark
Wendy Rathbone

Now Available!
*The long-awaited sequel to **THE FOUNDLING!***
In the eagerly-awaited sequel to Wendy Rathbone's homoerotic romance "The Foundling," Diego and Alec meet new challenges in private and from the outside world. Diego is being investigated by the local police for murder. Meanwhile, Alec's amnesia and the trauma of his kidnapping by white slavers continue to plague him. And the danger to Alec is not yet over.

Distracted by their new love, both men fail to see certain threats until it is almost too late.

"Why do you keep doing this illegal business?" Now Alec's gaze turned toward him, open as the day and lit with a sad frenzy, a challenge. "You could go anywhere, do anything, be anyone."

Diego had asked himself that question on rare occasions. In truth, he got used to what he was, what he did. Even a dangerous known was perhaps preferable to the unknown. "People depend on me."

Alec shook his head, but smiled a little as he said, "That's so weak." He leaned forward, over the arm of the chair, and put his shaking hand on the back of Diego's head. The kiss was cool, lingering, moist with salt. When Alec pulled back, he said almost matter of factly, "It's like there's sharks and there's goldfish and one can't decide to become the other."

Diego was still stunned by the kiss. But the words hit him hard. In them was the unfair conjecture of a locked fate. He believed in making his own fate...or luck. Did Alec think only one kind of man lived inside him and that was all there was to it? To life? It hurt. Badly.

Diego sat back on his heels, catching himself with his hands on the smooth, plank floor. "So, Alec, which am I?"

Alec frowned.

Diego said, "I made choices in my life. I made them No one made them for me. If I need to be strong I'm strong. If I need to be vicious I can be that too. So what? I'm stuck there? In a pattern, a role...with no free will?"

Alec watched him inquisitively now.

"Because," Diego went on, "I'm solely responsible for my actions. Me. Could you say the same of the shark?"

They both waited, the silence covering them in muggy discomfort.

"You think you understand me?" Diego finally asked.

My House Is Full of Whispers
Wendy Rathbone

Ten erotica short stories by Wendy Rathbone - former winner of the prestigious WRITERS OF THE FUTURE contest!

Leda has not one beautiful man, but two. Kale enters a secret world in a wealthy man's basement. Noah is in love with a man who hates sex. Dina lives next door to a famous Hollywood director she secretly loves. Dorian has a sixteen year old female student coming onto him. Tara is haunted by an erotic ghost. Young Dimitri is kidnapped by lecherous men. And more.

Author's Preface

When I wrote these stories, I deliberately set out to gently break down certain barriers, and I've certainly broken taboos. Do I care? No. This is fantasy at its purest level. The stories are never meant to be political statements, nor do they make any attempt at political correctness, and there is little consideration for safe sex. While I definitely condone safe sex, my stories come from fictional realities in my head where safe sex is not much of a concern because, well, it's imaginary and it's fiction!

For me, these stories are meant as little poetic erotic ramblings merely to stir the flames of desire, nothing more. They are pure fantasy and therefore to be enjoyed as such. Every story is erotic in nature, meant to titillate, some more explicit than others. Some of the stories are light, some are darker. I invite the reader to a feast of diversity and delight.

One reader commented: "...some of the most beautifully written erotica since Anais Nin!"

From the author: www.eyescry.com/html/publications.htm
On Amazon: http://www.amazon.com/House-Full-Whispers-Wendy-Rathbone-ebook/dp/B00IJK3G04/

UNEARTHLY
by Wendy Rathbone

A Collection of
Award-Winning Poetry

Intro by the Author: This book contains all my out of print chapbooks (mini-collections of an author's work usually published by smaller presses.)

The chapbooks published within include:
Moon Canoes, published by Dark Regions Press, 1994
(Im)mortal, published by Shadowfire Press, 1996
Scrying The River Styx, published by Anamnesis Press, 1999
Autumn Phantoms, published by Flesh and Blood Press, 2000
Dreams of Decadence Presents: Wendy Rathbone, published by DNA Publications 2002
Dancing in the Haunted Woodlands, published by Yellow Bat Review, 2003
Vampyria, published by Eye Scry Publications, 2005

She Sleeps With Vampires
She sleeps with vampires
courting velvet breaths
poem-dreams
chill-stopped hearts

Wrapped in her arms
like teddy bear thoughts
purple lips trembling
at her quiet throat
they love her more than
somber rain
more than autumn
more than ash-soft hearths of night.

From the author: www.eyescry.com/html/publications.htm
On Amazon: http://www.amazon.com/Unearthly-Wendy-Rathbone-ebook/dp/B00B0MTIZK/

COYOTE
Della Van Hise

A Novel of Love, Honor and Personal Sacrifice...

When River Willows is accused of a murder she didn't commit, her life takes a turn toward the sanctuary of a world existing at right-angles to our own. Combining the mysticism of martial arts and the romantic conflict of a young woman torn between two powerful men, COYOTE takes the reader on an epic journey of dangerous secrets, military cover-ups, and the infinite heart of the peaceful warrior.

"So who's Coyote?" I asked, trying to ignore the effect he was having on me. "You?"

Steale laughed easily, though it did little to hide the torment behind that mask of indifference he wore so well.

"Coyote's a scavenger, Jack of all trades. The Native Americans call him the trickster - the one who brought chaos down on the world." He shrugged as if altogether unconcerned. "Original sin."

"Is that what you are?" I asked, keeping it light despite the growing knot my stomach. "Original sin?"

He kept his profile to me, eyes straight ahead as he drove. "Sure you want to know?"

I couldn't help wondering if I had cornered the coyote, or if the clever trickster had cornered me.

By the author of **KILLING TIME** – without a doubt the most controversial **STAR TREK** novel ever published!
From the Author: www.eyescry.com/html/publications.htm
On Amazon: http://www.amazon.com/Coyote-Della-Van-Hise-ebook/dp/B00DRNEINC/

SONS OF NEVERLAND
an erotic vampyre novel by
Della Van Hise

"The virtuosity shown here is only the beginning of a pyrotechnic talent unfolding into the hidden dimensions of the human and nonhuman spirit."
-Jacqueline Lichtenberg

"Sensual! Sexy! Surreal!"
-North County Times

"A literary triumph where the undead have more heart & soul than the living."
-The Readers

"What Sons of Neverland resembled to me was the creative hagiographies of Nikos Kazantzakis, where a few stylized characters deliver a message that goes way beyond the parameter of the characters themselves. And much like Kazantzakis, this book zones on the question of immortality. However, this is not just the decadent historical immortality of the long-lived vampire, it is immortality as a change in one's perception. This is the story behind the story, delivered by characters that are hyper-real - each one loaded with symbolism. Sons of Neverland will have you filled, even brimming over with the sense of Mysterium Tremendum et Fascinans. Go there for a full helping of the numinous." (A Reviewer on Amazon!)

Set against a backdrop of contemporary culture, SONS OF NEVERLAND explores the universal questions of life & death, sex & love - the most crucial challenges every human being faces - through the eyes of the immortal vampire.

Readers have compared SONS OF NEVERLAND to the works of Anne Rice, Carlos Castaneda, and Anais Nin. One reader summed it up as follows: "SONS OF NEVERLAND is one of the most erotic books I've ever read. I found it totally uplifting regardless of the gritty story In the end, it made me realize that light can't exist without darkness. Thank you for a truly exceptional read!" (Charlene J.)

A shorter version of this book was published in TOMORROW MAGAZINE, under the title "Kiss of the Black Angel." The novel in its entirety was published as a limited first edition under the title "Ragged Angels."

YEAR OF THE RAM
Della Van Hise

Year of the Ram was described by one reviewer as... "A spacefaring gay romance full of love, angst, and longing."

Only after Star Commander Morgan Diego becomes an exile as a result of a Galaxy Corps political blunder does he begin to realize how much he valued the companionship of his second in command - the mysterious Lucien, an Alfarian who is more elven than human, with peculiar powers & abilities which begin to unfold as he, too, realizes what he has lost.

Separated by circumstance from his former life, Morgan is thrust into a world where he must survive by his wits. When he meets a peculiar little old man calling himself Kim Le, Morgan finds himself in a situation where he is required to master The Art - not only a form of human & extraterrestrial martial arts, but a way of living and being that will alter his life forever.

At the temple, he is introduced to his new teacher, another Alfarian who begins to steal his heart - a heart which is already promised to Lucien. Torn and conflicted, Morgan struggles with the world he left behind and the world he now inhabits.

Beginning to believe he may never again return to his ship and to the friends and loved ones he left behind, he is all the more frustrated and heartbroken when a new Master arrives at the temple: a man to whom Morgan is immediately drawn both mentally and physically, a man who is strikingly familiar... yet utterly alien.

Year of the Ram is a fully-fleshed novel, approximately 97000 words, with a focus on the love story and romance angle. Set against a science fiction milieu, it explores the infinite possibilities of the human and alien heart. Sexual content is explicit, though is not the primary focus of the novel.

For those who like a romance that forces its characters to contemplate the ecstasies AND the agonies of love... you will enjoy *Year of the Ram* immensely.

From the Author:
http://www.eyescry.com/html/publications.htm

On Amazon:
http://www.amazon.com/Year-Ram-Della-Van-Hise-ebook/dp/B003YOSCKO/

TEACHINGS OF THE IMMORTALS
by Mikal Nyght
So... You Want To Live Forever?
The teachings are presented as brief vignettes in no particular order of importance. This is not a book you read from start to finish in a single night. It is a grimoire of self-creation, intended to be contemplated slowly so as to be assimilated wholly. Pick it up and turn to a page at random. Where your eyes come to rest on the page is your lesson for the day. Go no further until you have assimilated the lesson totally.

The teachings are seduction as much as instruction. This is the way of The Dark Evolution.

Two Brief Excerpts...
The Ruby Slippers
The danger of the consensual continuum is that its natural gravity exists at the lowest common denominator of human experience, and because of this it will automatically make you forget those elusive truths you've fought to learn, and before you know it you're lost in petty dramas again, sinking into the mire of old familiar scripts.

The only way to overcome this is to be continually cavorting with worlds and events beyond human experience, journeying into the unknown so that it can become known, expanding knowledge and awareness to become more than you were, bringing back from the Dreaming those secrets which will teach you how to use the ruby slippers to transport yourself over the rainbow to the vampyre wizard's secret lair.

Perception
This is the nature of reality: to be precisely what perception dictates, as solid and whole as your interpretation of it, or as changeable and eternal as you permit it to be.

It wasn't knowledge god tried to keep from Man, you see. It was perception, for perception alone has the power to destroy god and obliterate comfortable consensual realities to create unending immortality.

Take the apple, my embryonic children. Nibble its red red flesh. Open your vampyre eyes so you may finally begin to See.

From the Author: www.immortalis-animus.com
On Amazon: http://www.amazon.com/Teachings-Immortals-Mikal-Nyght-ebook/dp/B00C2HY5WS/

Eye Scry Publications
A Visionary Publishing Company
www.eyescry.com/html/publications.htm